P9-EDZ-196

He felt responsible for her.

What happened with his car only strengthened that belief. Someone had tampered with the brakes and Chloe could have been seriously hurt...or killed. He shuddered at the thought.

She laid her hand on his shoulder. "You're upset about your car, aren't you? We knew this could be a dangerous assignment. We're in a dangerous business."

T.J. stared into those glittering eyes and wanted to lose himself in them, to forget where they were for a few minutes at least. He wished they were anyplace but here in the middle of a case heating up. He grazed his forefinger across her cheek. "I should have been in my car," he whispered.

For a moment he allowed himself to focus totally on her. The house faded from his consciousness, and it was only Chloe and him, together in their own private world.

Then he heard the noise he dreaded—footsteps, approaching in the dark.

Books by Margaret Daley

Love Inspired Suspense

So Dark the Night
Vanished
Buried Secrets
Don't Look Back
Forsaken Canyon
What Sarah Saw
Poisoned Secrets
Cowboy Protector
Christmas Peril
  "*Merry Mayhem*"
§*Christmas Bodyguard*
 Trail of Lies
§*Protecting Her Own*
§*Hidden in the Everglades*
§*Christmas Stalking*
 Detection Mission
§*Guarding the Witness*
 The Baby Rescue
 Bodyguard Reunion

*The Ladies of
   Sweetwater Lake
†Fostered by Love
††Helping Hands
   Homeschooling
**A Town Called Hope
§Guardians, Inc.
ΩCaring Canines

Love Inspired

*Gold in the Fire
**A Mother for Cindy*
**Light in the Storm*
 The Cinderella Plan
**When Dreams Come True*
 Hearts on the Line
*Tidings of Joy
 Heart of the Amazon
†*Once Upon a Family*
†*Heart of the Family*
†*Family Ever After*
 A Texas Thanksgiving
†*Second Chance Family*
†*Together for the Holidays*
††*Love Lessons*
††*Heart of a Cowboy*
††*A Daughter for Christmas*
***His Holiday Family*
**A Love Rekindled
***A Mom's New Start*
Ω*Healing Hearts*
Ω*Her Holiday Hero*

MARGARET DALEY

feels she has been blessed. She has been married more than thirty years to her husband, Mike, whom she met in college. He is a terrific support and her best friend. They have one son, Shaun. Margaret has been writing for many years and loves to tell a story. When she was a little girl, she would play with her dolls and make up stories about their lives. Now she writes these stories down. She especially enjoys weaving stories about families and how faith in God can sustain a person when things get tough. When she isn't writing, she is fortunate to be a teacher for students with special needs. Margaret has taught for more than twenty years and loves working with her students. She has also been a Special Olympics coach and has participated in many sports with her students.

BODYGUARD REUNION

MARGARET DALEY

◆ HARLEQUIN® LOVE INSPIRED® SUSPENSE

If you purchased this book without a cover you should be aware
that this book is stolen property. It was reported as "unsold and
destroyed" to the publisher, and neither the author nor the
publisher has received any payment for this "stripped book."

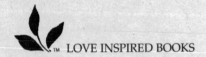 LOVE INSPIRED BOOKS

Recycling programs
for this product may
not exist in your area.

ISBN-13: 978-0-373-04207-4

BODYGUARD REUNION

Copyright © 2014 by Margaret Daley

All rights reserved. Except for use in any review, the reproduction
or utilization of this work in whole or in part in any form by any
electronic, mechanical or other means, now known or hereafter
invented, including xerography, photocopying and recording, or in
any information storage or retrieval system, is forbidden without
the written permission of the editorial office, Love Inspired Books,
233 Broadway, New York, NY 10279 U.S.A.

This is a work of fiction. Names, characters, places and incidents are
either the product of the author's imagination or are used fictitiously, and
any resemblance to actual persons, living or dead, business establishments,
events or locales is entirely coincidental.

This edition published by arrangement with Love Inspired Books.

® and TM are trademarks of Love Inspired Books, used under license.
Trademarks indicated with ® are registered in the United States Patent
and Trademark Office, the Canadian Trade Marks Office and in other
countries.

www.Harlequin.com

Printed in U.S.A.

Trust in the Lord with all thine heart; and lean not unto thine own understanding. In all thy ways acknowledge him, and he shall direct thy paths.
—*Proverbs* 3:5–6

To my husband, Mike. I love you.

ONE

Her first day on the job as a bodyguard for the Zimmermans and Chloe Howard already wanted to quit. In a limousine heading for the Dallas Community Christian Church, Chloe sat next to her client, Mary Zimmerman. Across from her, T. J. Davenport guarded Mary's husband, Paul. If Kyra Hunt, her employer at Guardians, Inc., had told her she would be working with T. J. Davenport, she would have declined the assignment. Instead, she would be around the man for the entire month of the Zimmermans' book tour.

Chloe kept her gaze trained out the side window, but occasionally felt the brush of T.J.'s dark gaze. He was probably trying to figure out how to back out of this assignment, too.

She'd worked with him nine years ago when he was a Secret Service agent and she was a police officer for the Dallas Police Department. From the beginning she'd been attracted to him, and when they had started dating, the attraction had grown into love—or so she'd thought. But his job had taken him away, and now she'd discovered he was back in Dallas, no longer a Secret Service agent.

The limo driver turned onto the road that curved up to the covered vestibule of a megachurch, where they would exit the vehicle. People crammed the entrance, waiting for the couple to arrive. Even on this windy, cold day, a large crowd was here, hoping to get a glimpse of the couple whose book, *Taking Back America,* had rocketed to number one on the *New York Times* bestseller list. This was the third such appearance by the Zimmermans, who wrote about putting God back into daily life. Off-duty police had roped off a path for the Zimmermans to the double glass doors, and each officer had taken up a post every few feet to hold the throng back.

Was it enough? Whoever had targeted Mary and Paul at their second stop in the book tour could be in the multitude waiting for them to climb from the car. So far, no description had been obtained of the person or persons in Paris, Texas, who had thrown stink bombs into the gathering, scattering everyone. Mary had nearly been trampled before her husband had gotten to her. Knowing what Mary and Paul stood for and the effect it must have had on them tightened Chloe's gut. That incident had led to the Zimmermans' publisher hiring two bodyguards for the third stop and the rest of their book tour.

Chloe straightened, scanning the area through the windows while T.J. did the same, his large body poised and alert. The Zimmermans had only reluctantly agreed to protection, not totally convinced there was a threat against them. They'd always had dissenters and had even received hate mail. A particular nasty letter had arrived at their first stop in Longview, Texas, and might be tied to the incident in Paris.

Chloe had wanted to sneak the couple into the church through a back way, but the Zimmermans didn't want to go that far. They wanted to be accessible to the people who had come to hear them speak. She'd tried to convince the pair of the potential danger, and to her surprise, T.J. had agreed with her.

Their parting in the past had been intense, filled with anger and hurt. He'd wanted to continue with a long-distance relationship. She'd seen too many of those fail—like her parents' marriage with her dad in the navy and gone a good part of the year.

As she did a final check of the huge crowd before exiting the limousine, her gaze collided briefly with T.J.'s. Not one emotion showed on his face, creating what she had come to think of as his professional facade. Cold. Determined. At one time she'd known a side to him apart from work. His laughter and smiles had always fulfilled a need in her for more of that in her life. There had been little of that growing up with a mother who hadn't been happy her husband was gone so much.

Chloe had even begun to picture what it would be like married to him—the children they would have. She'd wanted a family since she'd worked as a teenager in the church nursery each Sunday. She'd fallen in love with caring for children. No, she wasn't going to think about what could have been with T.J. if circumstances had been different.

She quickly focused on Mary Zimmerman, who had insisted on being addressed by her first name. "We need to escort you inside as fast as we can. Keep moving. I'll be right behind you."

Dressed in a powder-blue suit with a pencil skirt, Mary uncrossed her legs, her forehead crinkling. "But these people are out here because they want to hear us speak. The seating inside has been sold-out for weeks. I can't ignore them when they took the time to come here."

"Someone in that crowd might want to harm you and your husband." T.J. slid closer to the door and gripped the handle. "Stink bombs may seem like a prank, but two people were hurt seriously enough to go to the hospital. Thankfully you all took care of those hurt, but if your husband hadn't gotten to you when he did, you might have needed to be hospitalized, too."

"But what if that was kids in Paris and our publisher overreacted? I know that sort of thing happened at my high school several times when I was a teenager." Paul Zimmerman took his wife's hand.

T.J. looked from Mary to Paul. "How about the threatening letter delivered to your hotel in Longview? Another teenage prank?"

Chloe swiveled her attention to T.J. He plowed his fingers through his thick, wavy black hair—one of the few habits she'd noticed before that indicated he was worried about something.

T.J. continued, "It described in detail what he wanted to do with you two, beginning with torture. That doesn't sound like a teenager. I've read some of your hate mail, and that one had a different feel to it."

He'd read some of the Zimmermans' hate

mail? When? How had he gotten it? She'd been assigned this case only hours ago. Other than being apprised of what had happened in Longview and Paris, she had nothing else to go on. Not even the hate letter they'd received in Longview. Time had been limited when she had met with Kyra this morning.

The thought that T.J. knew more than she did irritated her, but mostly she felt she didn't have all the information to do the best job possible because this job had come up so suddenly. When this event was over, she would have a few choice words with the man. Just because he'd been the team leader on the one case they had worked on together didn't mean that was the situation now. The only way she could do this job was to be totally professional and an equal partner.

Paul frowned. "This is curtailing our mission to reach the masses as personally as we can, and that certainly isn't from behind bodyguards and police lines. They need to see we aren't afraid to fight for what is right."

"Honey, maybe that's the point of the

threats. To keep us from connecting with the people." Even in the midst of a tense situation, a smile graced Mary's lips. "The Lord is our protection, but our publisher will cancel this tour if we don't agree to—" she waved her hand toward Chloe and T.J. "—them being our bodyguards. I think spreading our message is too important to cancel the tour."

A long sigh escaped Paul's lips. "Fine, but I'm having a talk with the publishing house after this is over with. Let's go."

Chloe studied T.J.'s reaction to the declaration, and not one emotion crossed his face. She'd worked with him and knew that expression, but she'd also seen its opposite. When he'd been waiting for a chance to protect someone on the level of the vice president and finally got his promotion, she wouldn't move to Washington to be with him. Anger, hurt and disappointment had swirled between them that day.

She'd had her reasons. He'd had his. They'd parted. After a few calls from T.J. trying to persuade her to come to Washington, she'd never heard from him again until this morning when Kyra had introduced her to her partner in this assignment.

Before he could catch her staring at him, Chloe busied herself with opening the door and exiting the limo. The wind whipped through her, its cold sting biting. She surveyed the crowd, looking for any potential threats. Too many people pressed together. Too many possibilities.

Cheers rose from the spectators, the din assailing Chloe's ears as the crowd closed in around the Zimmermans, who started toward the entrance. This beloved couple's message touched many people. Chloe herself was a fan of their grassroots movement to take back the family and this country. They were full of integrity, compassionate and straightforward in what was important. Who wouldn't believe in their ideas?

But someone out there wasn't a fan. And she knew firsthand how hate could fester, exploding outward to include everyone. She'd seen more than her share, to the point that she wondered how much longer she could do what she was doing. But this was what she was good at.

Chloe moved forward on Mary's right toward the massive double glass doors. T.J. took the left side of Paul, steering him through the people wanting to shake hands with the couple before they headed into the church.

Every sense on alert, Chloe kept her hand near her holstered gun. Something didn't feel right. Or was she confusing this with an assignment she'd had a year ago under similar circumstances? Her shoulder still ached where she'd taken a bullet defending her client.

Mary had stopped and leaned close to an older woman, taking her hand. "I'll be praying for you and your family."

Tears glistened in the fiftysomething spectator's eyes. "That means so much to me. I don't know what else to do anymore."

"Praying is important. I'll be addressing some of the issues you're dealing with today. I know our talk will be piped out here for the people who couldn't get seats." Mary lifted the rope standing between her and the woman. "But I'm sure we can find one extra place for you."

Chloe inched closer to Mary, especially as the crowd surged forward with the vacant spot left by the lady. Several people nearby shouted various problems they were dealing with, but the words jumbled into incoherent sentences.

"We need to keep moving," Chloe whispered to Mary while her full attention remained fixed on the throng. "Your husband is at the door waiting."

Mary nodded and replied to a few close to her as she shuffled forward, shaking hands with as many as she could.

They were only yards away from the entrance now. The feeling of being watched tickled up Chloe's spine, leaving goose bumps in its wake. She'd learned not to ignore that sensation. She glanced back, but couldn't tell anything because everyone's eyes were on them.

Then a middle-aged man, going bald, pushed past the off-duty officer and grabbed Mary, making her stop. "I want to sit inside, too. Take me."

Chloe stepped forward, putting herself between Mary and the man, forcing him to let go of her client and back away. Anger flashed across his face. Tension whipped down Chloe as others began to shout they wanted inside.

Mary smiled, although Chloe could see the corners of her mouth twitching from holding it in place. "I'm sorry. The fire codes are specific about how many people can be in the auditorium."

Finally, Mary and the older lady entered a large church foyer with lots of windows and skylights. Mary paused to talk to one of the coordinators to make sure someone took care of the lady and to see about letting the crowd outside stand in the foyer, where it was warmer.

Having no time to do a walkthrough beforehand, Chloe swept her gaze around her surroundings as she crossed the threshold, noting where everyone stood, where the doors and exit signs were, as the floor plan she'd seen indicated. "I don't think that's wise under the circumstances," she whispered to Mary, imagining the chaos that could cause.

The young coordinator called over an older gentleman, who must be the person in charge, and they talked together.

The man turned to Mary. "We'll try to accommodate as many as we can."

"Will they be able to hear our talk?"

"We can pipe your speech out into the foyer. But we can't fit everyone in here."

"I understand. I'd appreciate anything you can do to make it better for the people outside. Bless you for trying." Mary made her way toward her husband, taking his offered hand.

The love that flowed between them made Chloe wonder when she had given up on her dream of having a family—a husband who loved her like that and at least two children. But everyone she'd dated since T.J. hadn't been right, especially her last boyfriend,

Adam. He'd cheated on her. At least T.J. hadn't done that.

The noise of the crowd in the massive auditorium at the end of the lobby grew to a deafening roar the nearer they came. With every seat taken, there were over fifteen hundred cheering people here to listen to the Zimmermans. Chloe wouldn't relax until they were all back at the house where the couple was staying.

The young coordinator escorted the guest speakers toward the stage area. As the Zimmermans stepped out to greet the crowd, the people all rose, clapping and yelling. A wall of sound assaulted Chloe. As the audience finally quieted, Chloe stationed herself behind the Zimmermans, positioning herself so the lights didn't obscure her view of the spectators. Her quick glance took in where T.J. was. He tipped his head toward her, his signal he would take the left side of the auditorium while she cased the right. Even with her and T.J. each taking half the auditorium, it was hard to keep an eye on everyone since people crammed the place.

After the presentation by the Zimmermans, T.J. paced the room above the church auditorium like a bear he'd seen at the zoo. He should be used to waiting. It was a big part of his job, but this assignment was different—and all because Chloe Howard prowled the other side of the room. From the surprised look that had flashed across her face this morning before she masked it, he was sure she hadn't known he was the other bodyguard on this case.

In fact, he was positive she hadn't or she wouldn't have taken the case. Not after how they had parted nine years ago. He'd been falling in love with her when he'd been given a choice assignment to be part of the detail covering the vice president. He had been a Secret Service agent at the time, assigned to Dallas working counterfeiting cases and financial crimes, sometimes in coordination with the Dallas Police Department. He couldn't turn down a chance to move into the protection part of the United States Secret Service, a move that would make his career in the agency. He'd wanted Chloe to move to Washington and see if their relationship would grow into a lasting one. He'd known from his fellow agents how hard being a law enforcement officer could be on a marriage, and that a marriage would only survive if it was based on a deep friendship. He'd decided he would only marry once.

She wouldn't leave Dallas. Her widowed mother had been fighting cancer, going through chemo, and she'd needed Chloe. He'd understood that, but she also hadn't wanted to have a long-distance relationship. He'd realized it would be difficult, but he'd been willing to try it, even though he had trouble trusting others—collateral damage of his law enforcement days. He'd never found someone like Chloe. Was that the reason he'd decided to settle in Dallas when he'd left the Secret Service?

Now, having seen Chloe, he wondered at

the wisdom of asking to team up with her, even though she was an excellent bodyguard. From working with her nine years ago on a counterfeiting case in conjunction with the Dallas police, he'd seen her dedication, and that had impressed him enough to persuade her to go out with him after their assignment was over.

He turned from watching her out of the corner of his eye and peered out the only window in the room that overlooked the church entrance hall. Finally the crowd was thinning and soon they could leave. He'd feel better when they were back at the couple's temporary residence, the house of one of their good friends who was on vacation, although T.J. could never totally let down his guard. The chances of something happening increased during transport from one place to another.

He was still amazed the Zimmermans had had to be convinced to have two bodyguards. Today, at their talk, he'd sensed a person in the audience calculating how to get to the pair, but he hadn't noticed anyone who stood out. He'd learned, though, not to ignore that gut feeling. It had saved his life several times.

The couple might think the past threats had been pranks. They hadn't been. He glanced at them, talking with the organizers of the event. When he'd insisted on bringing Mary and Paul into the church the back way, they had told him they were in the Lord's hands and were safe.

He'd believed in God fervently at one time. Now he was at a crossroads in his life, especially concerning the important aspects of life. He was good at guarding people, but he'd become jaded in his job. He needed something more. That was the reason he'd resigned from the Secret Service after fourteen years and approached Kyra Hunt about going into partnership with her and expanding Guardians, Inc. While he took this assignment with Chloe, Kyra would consider his proposition of taking the business to the next level.

He sensed Chloe advancing toward him, although her footsteps were quiet. He glanced over his shoulder, locking gazes with her.

In the past those sea-green eyes had been warm with emotions developing between them. Now they were cold. Her demeanor was totally professional and reserved—at least where he was concerned. He had known going in that might be the situation, but he'd wanted the best female bodyguard as his partner. In that moment, though, he acknowledged he had wanted more. Were there lingering feelings?

A memory of their first kiss years ago taunted him, stirring emotions he'd tried to forget and thought he had. They hadn't been right for each other nine years ago. Why should now be any different?

"We should be able to leave in ten or fifteen minutes. I'd prefer to wait until most of the people have left before we do." T.J. assessed her long auburn hair pulled back in a ponytail and remembered a time when her hair had been chin length and straight. What else was different?

Chloe stiffened, but her expression remained blank.

"Is there a problem?"

She released a long breath. "No, I agree with your plan, but before you whisk *my* client anywhere, please inform me of your intentions. If this is going to work, we'll need to be equal partners. A *team*." Emphasizing the last word, she looked him directly in the eye and held his gaze as though waiting for him to challenge that claim.

"I totally agree, and I'm sorry I acted without consulting you after their presentation. However, there may be times when it'll be necessary for one of us to act and then explain. The lobby is still full of people from the crowd outside." He refused to break visual contact.

Her chin tilted up a fraction, and she squared her shoulders even more. But the look in her eyes, a stormy green like the sky right before a tornado struck, mellowed. "I know the only time we worked together you were the team leader and used to giving orders. My first priority will be Mary Zimmerman. I was hired to protect her. You were hired to guard her husband. I've been working for Guardians, Inc., for four years. I'm not a novice anymore." The tense set to her body relaxed. "I've changed since we knew each other."

He had changed, too. He realized if they were together very long on this assignment they would have to discuss their parting nine years ago, but with one glance around the room, he knew this wasn't the time or the place. "I know you aren't. I've read over the assignments you've done this past year. I'm impressed. That's why I asked for you. I felt a woman would be better suited for guarding Mary, so I contacted Kyra." He wouldn't go into the details about the possibility of buying into a partnership with Kyra for Guardians, Inc. He wouldn't be part of Guardians, Inc., if he and Chloe couldn't at least call a truce between them.

"You know my boss?" Her body visibly relaxed.

"Yes, I've known her since the first time I lived here. We've kept in touch through the years." And he'd asked from time to time about Chloe. Another tidbit he wouldn't tell her.

Chloe peered out the window, confusion clouding her eyes for a few seconds. "She didn't tell me. I didn't even know you would be guarding Paul."

"I told her not to say so because there was little time to get someone and I didn't want you to refuse before meeting the Zimmermans. There's so much that changed in nine years. I didn't want our past together to affect you taking the assignment."

She blinked several times.

"Their publisher didn't contact me about the job until late last night. So I went to Kyra early this morning and was glad to learn you were available."

"But—" she looked away again "—after what happened between us, I'm surprised."

A silence fell between them peppered with murmurs from Paul and Mary's conversation with the organizers. T.J. inched closer and lowered his voice. He touched her arm, not sure if she would yank away or not. She didn't. "We need to talk later. I don't want anything standing in the way of this partnership. I'm not the same man I was. Life has a way of redirecting your dreams."

Chloe opened her mouth, but instead pressed her lips closed before saying anything and fastened her attention out the window. An uncomfortable moment later, she said, "It looks like the crowd is gone. I'll feel better when we get them back to the house. Everything went well, but I couldn't shake…" Her eyebrows slashed downward.

"I got the feeling someone was out there watching the Zimmermans, waiting for the right moment."

She faced him. "I did, too, but then nothing happened, even with the last-minute change Mary insisted on with the crowd coming inside. I was beginning to wonder if my instinct was off. Generally, it isn't."

In that brief moment a connection sprang up between them as if their breakup had never occurred. "I don't think it is. Someone in the audience could have been casing the Zimmermans. Just because he did something at the first and second stops in the tour doesn't mean he will at this one. The security was tightened, and he might not have expected that."

Finally, as though she'd realized his hand was touching her, she stepped back. "You keep saying *he*. Is there a reason you think it's one man?"

He shook his head. "I need a way to refer to the person or persons since we don't have any names."

"I just want to make sure I know everything connected to this assignment. No clues to who is after them?"

"From what happened in Paris with the multiple stink bombs, I figure it's more than one person. But frankly, I know so little at this time." T.J. glanced at the pair they were guarding. "I'm concerned mostly about their lack of concern."

"It could lead to problems. Mary puts everyone else first."

"You know her?" T.J. kneaded his shoulder, aching from holding himself taut and ready to move at a second's notice. There was still tension with Chloe. He'd thought the past was just that—the past—that they could forge a working relationship because Chloe was good at her job.

"Not personally, but I know of her. I've read her books, and they have a great message. We need to put God's principles into action."

"In theory, the concepts they promote might work, but in practice we need more law enforcement officers and tougher laws." When he saw her forehead crease, he continued, "We should leave, but we'll talk later, and I'll make sure you know everything I do. There won't be any confusion with this assignment."

One of her perfectly arched eyebrows lifted, a smile flirting with her mouth. "Promise?"

He chuckled. "Yes, we made a good team once before. There's no reason why we can't now." Her smile gave him hope that they could at least work together.

"I suppose anything is possible."

"Let's get the Zimmermans to a more secure location. Okay?"

She nodded.

Turning toward the couple, T.J. said, "It's time for us to leave."

While the Zimmermans said goodbye to the organizers, T.J. withdrew his phone from his pocket and called the limo driver to pull the car around to the back exit. Now that the crowd was gone, the couple shouldn't mind going out that way. He let it ring five times, then it went to voice mail.

"The Zimmermans are ready to leave. We'll stay put until you call back." His grip on the cell tightened. That gut feeling he'd had earlier clamored against his skull, demanding to be heard.

Chloe watched him as he slipped his phone back into his pocket and evened out his expression. Although she wasn't as easy to read as in the past, it was clear when concern invaded her eyes.

He moved closer to her and whispered,

"The driver didn't answer. I'm going out to the parking lot to see what has happened. You stay here and guard the Zimmermans. I'll call you and let you know what's going on. Lock the door after I leave."

He started to turn away, but she grasped his arm. "I won't open that door unless you tell me it looks like it's going to rain. Okay?"

"Yes."

She didn't release her grip. "Be careful. I don't have a good feeling about this."

Just like I don't. Which only reinforced the suspicion something was wrong.

Nodding, he strode toward the exit, ushering the two organizers out of the room in front of him. The sound of the lock clicking into place didn't quiet the alarms going off in his mind. He could think of a hundred reasons the driver hadn't answered the call—most of them bad.

He left the church through the back door, his gaze sweeping the area around him before he stepped out into the cold February day. A brisk wind blew from the west, slamming against his torso as he headed around the side of the church where the driver was supposed to have parked the limousine. Fifteen yards away, he spied the car where it should be.

The windows were darkened, so when T.J. stared into the vehicle, he couldn't see the driver. Anywhere, inside or out.

Then T.J. noticed the tire nearest him had been slashed. From where he stood he could see the back one, too. Flat. His stomach clenched. Adrenaline pumped through his body as he pulled his gun from his holster. While he scanned the parking lot, he made his way to the limo. His heartbeat picked up speed as adrenaline flooded his system.

He circled the limo quickly. Two more flat tires. No one hiding behind the car. When he returned to the driver's side, he yanked open the passenger door. No one hiding there, either. Then he turned his attention to the front. When T.J. opened the door, there was no sign of the driver or where he might be.

T.J. pushed a button on the side panel,

then hurried to the back of the limo. When he lifted the trunk, his breath bottled in his lungs. He'd found the driver.

TWO

Chloe paced in the room above the auditorium. She should have heard from T.J. by now. This didn't bode well. Tension held her tighter with each minute that ticked away until she felt like a walking statue. When her cell rang, she came to a halt. It was T.J.'s phone calling.

"Yes?" she said with wariness. *Please let him be okay.*

"The driver was knocked out and locked in the trunk of the limousine. All the tires have been slashed. I'm coming into the church now with the driver. I wanted you to know what happened before I call the police." A slight breathlessness to his words indicated he was hurrying to get back to the room.

"I'll call. I know some people on the police

force." She disconnected and immediately placed a call to a detective who was a friend and filled him in on where they were and what had happened, then she called for an ambulance.

A knock cut through the sudden silence in the room as Mary and Paul listened to Chloe's conversation with Detective Rob Matthews. Paul started for the door.

"Don't! Let me." Sliding her phone into her pocket, then drawing her gun, Chloe hurried to cut him off. He stopped, his eyes huge as he looked from her to Mary.

"There was a problem at the limo. Someone knocked out the driver and slashed the tires." Chloe clasped the handle and motioned for Paul and Mary to stand in the corner, out of the line of fire. When they had moved, she asked, "Who is it?"

"T.J. here. It looks like it's going to rain." His deep, husky voice penetrated the barrier of wood between them.

The smooth sound of his words sent relief through her—and something else, a flutter deep in her stomach. She dismissed the re-action, chalking it up to being glad he was all right. She couldn't afford to fall for T.J. again. She unlocked the door and swung it open while keeping her gun ready at her side.

T.J. helped the stunned driver into the room as Chloe shut the door and threw the lock—not that it would stop someone really determined to get inside. In fact, she could probably pick the lock in under a minute.

Mary rushed from the corner with Paul right behind her. When she reached the driver, she waved her hand toward the near-est chair. "I've had some first-aid training. Let me check him."

The Zimmermans tended to the man, who responded to Mary's questions about how he felt as she looked into his eyes, then exam-ined the back of his head. When she probed with her fingertips, the young man winced.

"How long until the police and paramedics arrive?" T.J. asked Chloe, drawing her atten-tion to him.

"I called a friend, Rob Matthews, who is

on duty and will send some patrol officers.
He's on his way, too, but they'll get here first.
Maybe ten minutes out. Does the driver know
what happened?"

"He was groggy. I wanted to get in here before questioning him. I kept thinking it might
have been a diversion."

"It's been quiet."

Mary crossed the room to the counter where
there was a sink and wetted some paper tow-
els. As she made her way back to the driver,
Paul walked over to them, his color pale.

"What's going on?" His voice wavered.

"Not sure. At best, another harassment."
T.J. started for the driver and Mary.

"And the worst?" Paul followed.

"The attacker is out there waiting to do
something else, most likely to you and your
wife."

T.J.'s declaration caused Paul to falter.

Chloe grasped his arm and steadied him.
"That's why we're here. To protect you and
Mary." She looked toward T.J. and was com-
forted he was her partner. He exuded a self-

assurance that would keep the Zimmermans as composed as possible under the circumstances. She'd discovered that was important when events turned bad.

"What should we do?" Paul asked Chloe.

"Pray. The police are on the way. They'll check the surrounding area and the church. Right now it's best if we stay in here until we're given the all-clear sign from them." She schooled her voice into a calm, even tone.

"How are we getting back to the house?"

"I'll ask my detective friend to take us. The driver needs to be checked out by a doctor. The paramedics coming will take care of him. From the looks of it, he might have a concussion."

As T.J. paused next to the driver, Mary finished tending to the man with her limited resources. Chloe moved with Paul toward the trio. She needed to know what had happened to the driver.

"I think he'll be fine. He's coherent." Mary backed away while Paul wrapped his arms around her.

"Did you see who did this to you, Ben?" T.J. sat in a chair in front of the young man, whose dazed look had cleared.

Ben Johnson leaned against the table, cradling his head in one hand. "Not really. That parking space was one of the few left after I dropped y'all in front." Closing his eyes for a few seconds, he rubbed his fingers across his forehead. "I parked and sat in the car for a while before I decided to use the restroom. I came into the church, found the men's room then went back to the limo."

"Did you see anyone in the parking lot?"

"A large man came out of the restroom as I was going in, but otherwise no one else. I heard the general rumble from the auditorium and saw people down the hall toward the front of the church—I guess in the foyer."

"Can you describe the man coming out of the bathroom?" T.J. gripped the back of his chair.

"Big. Maybe six and a half feet. Dark hair. That's all I can remember. I wasn't really paying attention. The boss doesn't like us away from the limo for long. I was only gone five minutes." Ben swept his gaze across the group.

Chloe stepped next to T.J. "What happened when you went back to the car?"

"I saw the slashed tires on the left side and hurried to see how bad the damage was. All I could think was how mad my boss would be. The next thing I know someone hit me over the head. Everything is fuzzy after that. I vaguely remember being dumped in the trunk. I must have passed out."

"So you don't know where your attacker came from?" T.J. asked the driver, but he looked at Chloe.

She tore her gaze away and focused on Ben.

He squinted and stared off into space for a moment. "He must have come from behind the car next to the limo on the right side. I think."

"But you aren't sure?" Chloe asked as though she and T.J. had silently agreed to take turns with the questions.

"No. It happened fast."

"Can you describe the car on your right?" T.J. rose suddenly, invading her space.

Ben's eyes lit up. "Yes. I may not remember people, but I do remember what they drive. It was a red Mustang, last year's model. A beauty. The car gleamed."

"Anything else?" Chloe moved back several steps, her heartbeat increasing from T.J.'s nearness.

"There was a pine-tree air refresher hanging from the rearview mirror. I love the smell of pine."

Chloe's cell phone rang. She walked toward the window that overlooked the front of the church and answered a call from Rob. "What's going on?" Outside, three patrol cars pulled up to the entrance.

"The officers are there and will check out the church. I'll meet them there in ten with my partner. They'll let me know when it's safe for you all to come out."

"Thanks. We're in the room above the auditorium in front. I'll be able to see you pull up."

T.J. joined her as she put her cell back into her pocket. He looked at the police fanning out and heading into the building. "We don't have much to go on."

"Do you think the driver could be involved?"

"I don't think he's lying. There are no big tells. But some people are quite good at lying."

His shoulder brushed against hers when he shifted. The casual touch zipped through her, making her acutely aware of the man beside her at the window—almost as if only days had passed since they had been together instead of years. It disconcerted her, and she had to fight to think what she needed to say. "So I'll have Kyra check the company and driver out. But I don't see how the description of the car next to the limo will produce anything."

"While you were on the phone, Ben remembered the last three numbers of the license plate. It's probably nothing, but we should tell your detective friend about the Mustang."

"In other words, we're no closer to who or why someone is after the Zimmermans. Ben referred to the assailant as 'he.' Does he think it was a man who attacked him?"

"I didn't ask. I will, but Ben is over six feet tall and a hefty guy. To knock him out and stick him into the trunk would take someone large and capable of managing that physically."

"The man from the restroom?"

T.J. shrugged. "As you said, we have little to go on."

A movement out of the corner of her eye caught her attention. A black Crown Vic drove into the parking lot and stopped next to one of the patrol cars. Not far behind the police was the ambulance that pulled up to the door to the church. "Rob and his partner are here as well as the EMTs. I told Rob where we were. He'll let us know when it's safe for us to come out of the room."

T.J. massaged his nape, a frown marring the hard planes of his face. Although he wasn't classically handsome, his strong features gave off an air of capability and confidence. On closer examination, she realized he must have broken his nose between the time they had been together and now. How had it happened? Had there been other injuries? She didn't want to care, but she did.

Before she became fixated on that, she swung toward the window and observed her friend entering the building. But every part of her was strongly aware of the man standing next to her, their arms only inches apart as they watched the same thing.

"When we get back to the house, I'll need to contact the Zimmermans' publisher," he finally said as all the police disappeared inside.

"Are you going to recommend that the couple cancel the rest of the tour?"

"Yes. Their message might be important, but not if they are hurt or killed."

"They feel this country is at a crossroads. One road holds destruction. The other is a chance for salvation. They're out there fighting for us to take the right path. I'm not sure they'll quit."

"Then we'll have to do what we can to protect them."

He'd said *we'll*. She used to think of them in terms of we. She knew the danger of doing it now, but they had to form a solid partnership in order to protect the Zimmermans, who were clearly in danger. The more she and T.J. were a united front, the better Mary and Paul would be.

But at what cost to her feelings? When he'd left her to go to Washington, she'd been alone dealing with her mother and her chemo treatments. She'd missed her father, who had died two years before, and T.J. She'd never felt so alone. She couldn't go there again.

T.J. made his rounds of the two-story house, checking all the doors and window to make sure the place was locked up tight. It had been a long day, and the Zimmermans had retired early. Now all he and Chloe had to do was keep them alive. He'd worked with others in his duties as a Secret Service agent, and usually he was the lead. Chloe had made it clear, though, that they needed to be partners, and she was right.

When he entered the kitchen, the scent of perking coffee saturated the air. After the day he'd had, he would need the whole pot to keep going.

Chloe turned from the counter, a grin gracing her lips. "It's almost done."

For a few seconds that smile whisked away his worries. She'd made the day bearable; he'd known his back was covered. "I hope it's not decaf."

"What's the point in drinking coffee without the caffeine?"

He chuckled. "True. I remember you like your coffee like I do—strong and caffeinated." He recalled many things now that he was around her again. Her laugh—filled with so much joy. Her favorite dessert—anything with caramel. Her caring nature, especially for the underdog.

"It's strong. We'll have to take turns standing guard tonight, so when the coffee runs out, make some more."

"I'll take the first watch. Coffee won't keep me up when I do get a chance to sleep. I don't think anything will." He covered the distance to the pot and poured a mugful. "This house isn't as secure as it should be. I wish they weren't staying here, but they insisted. Their friend invited them to use it while he was away on a skiing vacation."

"We'll only be here a few more days, then on to San Antonio. Let's hope the next place they're staying is better."

"The alarm system is old and could be circumvented easily, not to mention the locks and door frames aren't as sturdy as I'd like."

Her large eyes trapped him. "Maybe we should try to find a more secure place tomorrow. Then both of us can stay up tonight. Just in case there's a follow-through with what happened today?"

He didn't remember her eyes being so green—like a peridot crystal—when they had been together before. "I'm a light sleeper. I'll leave the door open. We both need some sleep in order to do our jobs. Even no sleep for one night could impair our abilities."

Chloe took a sip. "I was thinking of stretching out in front of the entrance to the Zimmermans' bedroom. The easiest way to get to them is coming in the front door and up the stairs."

"I'll be planting myself on the stairs when not making my rounds. That way you can sleep in the room across the hall from the Zimmermans'. I can't imagine the hard floor being comfortable."

"I'm a light sleeper, too, so if you need help, just give me a holler."

The more he was around her, the more he realized they used to have a lot of things in common—but not enough for a commitment. "Wish we had a big dog right about now, but we'll have to rely on the alarm system."

"The one that's easily disarmed." Her eyes twinkled, a dimple appearing in her cheek.

Her look warmed him, although the old house they were staying in had a draft as if the cold wind blew right through it. "Afraid so." He cupped the mug between his hands and took a slow sip. "This might be a good time to talk. As crazy as this first day was, we may not have time later."

Putting her cup down, she leaned back with her hands grasping the counter on either side of her. "I would prefer we leave the past in the past. What happened nine years ago can't be changed."

She made it sound so easy. Just forget the past—the moments he'd shared with her, his decision to go into law enforcement rather than become a preacher and what his job had meant to him at the time. In the end it hadn't made any difference. They had gone their separate ways, and he needed to remember that.

"I made a choice to go to Washington—to take the promotion. I wanted you to come, but I understand why you didn't. You had other obligations. Looking back on that time, I don't think we were meant to be together. Sometimes people meet and begin to fall in love, but it doesn't work out. I don't want our past to interfere with the present." As he spoke to her, he wondered if he really believed it couldn't have worked out if circumstances had been different.

"I don't, either. I can put it behind me. Can you?" Her knuckles whitened as her grip tightened on the granite edge.

"Yes, because I may be working with Guardians, Inc., and I can't think of anyone I'd want more than you as a partner, if the need arises."

"Kyra is expanding?"

"Maybe. I've given her a proposal to consider."

She pushed off the counter. "What kind?" Wariness entered her voice.

"I have a lot of contacts for potential personnel and clients from my years working in the Secret Service. I'd buy into the business, and we would expand, hiring male bodyguards to complement the female ones already working for Guardians, Inc. I'll take over some duties from her. I think she wants to have more time with her family." T.J. swallowed some more of his drink, relishing it. She made a good cup of coffee.

"So you'd become my boss?" Her forehead crinkled; her mouth pinched into a frown.

"Yes. Can you work for me?"

Chloe tilted her head to the side, her gaze fastened on him as if studying him. "I don't know if I can. Working on a case with you is one thing. We've got a past—one serious enough that you wanted me to follow you to Washington and I asked you to stay in Dallas. You didn't. You made your choice."

"I'd been working for that promotion for five years. I thought when your mother was better, you'd come. I asked you to. Why didn't you?"

"I wanted to be more important to a man than a job. It's the past. I don't want to go through this again. No good will come of it."

"So we'll put the past in the past as you said and proceed forward?"

She nodded, stepping away from him.

"That's all I need to know." He finished the last few sips of his coffee.

"What made you quit the Secret Service? Nine years ago it was obvious your life revolved around your job." Tension threaded through each word.

"Probably the same reason you quit the police department. I needed a change." He busied himself pouring another cup of coffee. He couldn't tell her about the government figure he'd protected while the man had had an affair. After a while, he hadn't been able to look away as if nothing was wrong. He believed in marriage and wanted to get married only once in his life. When his respect for the man had plummeted, he'd realized that it was time for him to seek employment elsewhere.

"When you feel up to telling me the whole story, I'm willing to listen." Her expression neutral, she passed him and headed toward the dining room. "I'll do a walk-through, then go up to the bedroom across from the Zimmermans. Wake me in four hours."

He watched her leave, then turned off the light and positioned himself at the bay window in the breakfast nook. Stepping close, he cracked the blinds open to survey the area outside. With all the security lights on, there were still pockets of shadows that could conceal a person from the patio to the wooden fence that surrounded the half-acre backyard. He had a bad feeling about this house. Good thing they were moving to San Antonio soon. He had a better place in mind for the Zimmermans to stay there, and the fewer people who knew the couple's plans, the better to keep them safe during their off hours.

Now all he and Chloe needed to do was get the Zimmermans to San Antonio safely.

Before falling into bed, Chloe walked toward the window at one end of the upstairs hallway. She tried to dismiss the conversation she'd had with T.J. She couldn't. When her mother had gone into remission, she'd actually considered resigning from the police force and going to Washington, D.C., to be with T.J.

But as she'd taken care of her mom, she'd seen the sadness and hurt she had held inside for years. While her mother had struggled with her battle with cancer, she had shared her disappointment in her marriage to a captain in the navy, who had been at sea for half their marriage, and how alone she'd felt for years. She hadn't wanted to end up like her mother—married to a man married to his job. She'd never contacted T.J. and refused his calls. She wouldn't settle for anything but what she deserved—a man who totally loved her and put her first rather than a career. She wasn't sure about T.J.'s true feelings. He'd left because of his career—like her father.

Chloe approached the window, keeping the overhead light off so she could see better when she looked out. The security lamp on this side of the house illuminated every crevice. She made her way to the other end and studied the terrain more carefully because the soft glow didn't cover every patch of ground. She started to turn away and go to bed when a movement out of the corner of her eye seized her full attention.

Someone was out there.

THREE

Chloe whirled away from the hallway window and ran to the stairs. As she descended, she drew her gun. "T.J., we've got a visitor." She shouted the words and raced for the alarm system to turn it off so she could go outside.

"Where?" T.J. rushed into the foyer, his weapon in his hand.

"Right side of house." Heart pounding, she punched in the off code, then hurried toward the front door at the same time he did. "I'll check outside. You stay in here and guard the Zimmermans." She reached for the handle first.

Her comment stopped him. He let his arm drop back to his side, a frown slashing his face. "I'm bigger. More capable of stopping an assailant."

"We're not going to get into an arm-wrestling match right now. I won't jump the person." She pulled open the door, narrowing her gaze on him. "I'm using my gun."

He charged out the entrance. "So am I. Lock the door, turn on the alarm and call the police."

Short of tackling him and knocking him out, Chloe had no other choice but to do as he said. But when this was over with, he would hear from her. She didn't need protecting, too.

She flipped the lock in place, then stabbed in the code to turn the alarm back on. Anger and frustration surged through her veins. Pushing those emotions down, she called her detective friend.

"You wanted to know if anything unusual happens. T.J. is outside trying to apprehend an intruder." She gave him the address.

"On my way."

As she hung up, she hurried up the stairs to check on the Zimmermans and let them know what was happening. When she knocked on their bedroom door, no one called out or let her in. She heard something hit the floor and reached for the knob.

Gun drawn and up, T.J. crept around the right side of the house, his full concentration on protecting his client. A picture of Chloe's furious face taunted his attention for a couple of seconds until he shoved it away. He'd deal with her anger later. His first priority was keeping everyone safe, including Chloe, whether she liked it or not.

A dog barked in the still of night—probably two or three houses away. His nerves taut, T.J. rounded the corner, ready to duck if shot at. He searched the shadows. Something moved beside a holly bush against the eight-foot fence. A man darted out from behind the foliage and ran toward the backyard.

T.J. gave chase, his strides lengthening. The intruder headed for the rear of the property, glancing over his shoulder at T.J., then sprinting faster.

T.J. increased his speed, cutting the distance between them. He catalogued the man's build—over six-and-a-half feet tall, slim, gangly, his limbs disproportionate to the rest of him, reminding T.J. of an octopus.

The intruder lunged for the top of the fence, trying to hoist himself over it. T.J. leaped toward him and grabbed his legs as the man dangled half on this side of the property. T.J. yanked hard and the trespasser fell into him, sending them both crashing backward. T.J. hit the ground first with the intruder landing on top of him.

The air swooshed from T.J.'s lungs. His head bounced against the ground, causing the world to spin before his eyes. The hard impact wrenched the gun from his hand, and his Glock flew across the grass.

The man rolled off T.J. Scrambling for his weapon, T.J. drew in a breath. But the prowler barreled into T.J. before he could grab his gun.

Chloe twisted the Zimmermans' bedroom door handle. Locked. "Mary. Paul. Open up." She threw her shoulder against the bar-

rier between her and her client. Pain radi-
ated through her body as she hit the door
again. Solid. Not budging. She stepped away
to shoot the lock.

"Coming. Coming," came Paul's deep
husky voice through the wood.

Chloe poised, ready at a second's notice to
react if he was being forced to let her in.

When he opened the door finally and stuck
his head out of the gap in the entrance, worried lines mixed with the exhaustion on his
face, his eyes blinking at the dazzling light
in the hallway. "What's wrong?"

"What was that crashing sound?"

"When I got out of bed, I bumped into an
end table. Why are you waking us up?" He
shook his head as though to wake himself
totally.

"There's a prowler outside. T.J. has gone to
check on the situation while I secure you two.
I need to come in and check your bedroom."

"No one's in here. I'd know."

"Humor me."

He flipped on the overhead light and

stepped to the side to allow her to pass. Lying in bed, Mary groaned and hid her face as illumination flooded the room.

"She took a sleeping pill. After what happened today, she didn't think she would get to sleep any other way." Dressed in a long robe, Paul moved toward the bed. "What do you need us to do?"

"You two need to get up in case I have to move you quickly." Chloe made a tour of the room, inspecting the closet and the connected bathroom. She stopped at the window and peered out the front of the house before checking to make sure it was locked. Satisfied no intruder was in the room, she crossed to the door. "Get dressed. I'll be out in the hall."

The muscles in her neck and shoulder taut, Chloe paced the corridor, examining the stairs and foyer below each time she passed them. Finally, when Mary and Paul left their bedroom, Chloe glanced at her watch. It had been ten minutes since T.J. had gone outside. She didn't like not knowing what was going on.

What if something happened to him? No, I won't think about that. T.J. can take care of himself. He's been protecting people longer than me. He's in Your hands, Lord.

The couple approached Chloe. Mary leaned against her husband, trying to wake up.

"What do we do now?" Paul asked, his arm around his wife.

"Sit down there—" Chloe gestured toward an area where their backs would be against the wall "—and if I tell you to move, do so immediately. Don't be alarmed. I'm turning off the hallway light so I can check outside and see what's happening."

She inspected the ground where she'd seen the intruder on the side of the house. Nothing. Where was T.J.? The prowler? If he ran from T.J., he would go for the backyard most likely. She flipped the hallway light on again, then entered a bedroom overlooking the rear.

The sight of a tall, thin man pouncing on a figure on the ground stiffened her. She leaned closer to see what was going on by the fence, the security lights not quite reaching the place where two men wrestled, rolling away from her view. The urge to go out and help was overpowering, but her job was to stay with the Zimmermans.

One last time, she searched the darkness at the back of the yard. The night shadowed the pair enough she couldn't tell what was going on. T.J. had had some of the best training in the world, but she hated the helplessness she felt. She shook it off and hurried toward the hallway. She needed to get Mary and Paul into the closet under the staircase—no windows and only one way in. That way she would be able to know if someone breached the lower level right away and defend them better until the police arrived.

T.J. threw a punch that connected with the intruder's jaw. The man returned it with a right uppercut, sending T.J. staggering back against the fence. The guy rushed in, pinning T.J. then pounding his fists into his stomach and torso. One. Two. Three jabs. The breath left his lungs. Lightheaded, he blocked the next assault and brought his knee up into his assailant. The man dropped to the ground, groaning. T.J. hammered him until the prowler went still.

T.J. wanted this to end. Still feeling dazed, he stumbled toward the place where his gun lay. An iron grip on his left leg, then a sharp jerk, sent him down. He shook off the assailant's hand and scrambled away, then struggled to his feet and faced his opponent. The man's features were obscured by the dark. The man drew himself up tall, his arms held out from his body as he sidled to the right. T.J. mimicked his moves, taking a reprieve in order to inhale deep, fortifying breaths.

"The police are on the way. I'm not letting you leave." T.J. made a full circle. The sound of the intruder's raspy breathing wafted to him. "You aren't getting away. You might as well make it easy for yourself and give up."

The prowler cackled. "I haven't done anything wrong. You attacked me. I welcome the police."

"You're trespassing on private property."

"You aren't going to stop me from getting my story."

Maybe the guy had hit T.J. one time too many. "Story?"

"Yes, I work for the *Texas Inquirer News.*"

"That's great. You can tell the police." In the distance a siren blared, a welcome sound. T.J. angled closer to his Glock, slicing a glance toward it.

In that split second, the man rushed T.J., taking him to the ground and rolling toward the gun. He'd never lost his gun, and he wouldn't let this be the first time.

The prowler kept reaching toward T.J.'s Glock. Inches from it, T.J. knocked the lanky guy's arm away, lurched across the short space and latched on to his weapon. With all his strength, he shoved the man away from him and swung the gun around, aiming it at the intruder's chest.

"Don't move." T.J. scooted back, then rose, keeping his Glock trained on the prone man.

The siren stopped, not far from the house. In spite of the cold air, sweat drenched T.J. The sound of the gate opening reverberated through the air, quickly followed by someone shouting, "Police!"

The prowler pushed to his feet, the security light illuminating the fury on his thin face. "Help. This man is going to kill me."

T.J. suppressed the urge to laugh, because until the police could straighten this out, he would be suspected, too.

"Drop the gun," the first of the two officers said, his own weapon on T.J.

T.J. followed his order and then raised his hands. "I'm T. J. Davenport. This man is trespassing."

With the patrol cars' lights flashing in the driveway, Chloe stood on the porch with Detective Matthews as two officers led T.J. and the intruder from the backyard. Both of them had their hands cuffed behind them.

She might be mad at T.J. for cutting her off and rushing outside after the prowler, but the sight of his cuts, his rumpled clothing and the bits of dead grass in his hair and on his sweatshirt emphasized she'd fared better than he had. She could take care of herself in most situations, but after one look at the size of the intruder, she had to admit in this case she might not have been able to. She gave a wry smile. Maybe she did have limitations.

But with the Lord all things are possible. You kept us safe. Thank You.

Rob stepped forward, waving his hand toward T.J. "He's the good guy. You can release him."

"Oh, please keep them on him for a few more minutes," Chloe whispered behind Rob.

Her friend chuckled. "Behave, Chloe."

The police officer took the handcuffs off T.J. "What do you want us to do with the other one?"

"I want to talk to him, then you can take him to the station," Rob said as he descended the steps.

Rubbing his wrists, T.J. plodded up the stairs to the top of the porch, where Chloe stood. "Where are Mary and Paul?"

"In the living room with an officer. They're safe."

"Good, because I want to be in on this interrogation." T.J. backed down several steps but glanced over his shoulder. "And I heard the crack about keeping the handcuffs on me."

Serves him right for playing the macho male. She presented an innocent expression. "You okay? You should be checked out by a doctor."

He turned toward Rob and the intruder. "I'm fine. It's happened before. Don't worry."

"I'm not. You know how to take care of yourself," Chloe fired back, not wanting him to think she had been worried about him. *But I was. Yeah, and that's the problem. My focus needs to be on Mary and Paul, not T.J.*

Though she tried not to, Chloe slanted a look toward T.J., his strong jaw set in a hard line, his usually neat and professional medium-length black hair messy from wrestling with an assailant. A vision of her running her hand through that hair was quickly replaced with another memory of the touch of his day-old beard beneath her fingers as she framed his face and leaned in to kiss…

Chloe shook the thoughts from her mind. That was the past. T.J. had made it clear that he had no room for a wife in his life, and then he'd flown to Washington to guard the vice president. She made a mistake only once— never twice.

"What were you doing here?" Rob asked the tall, lanky man, dragging Chloe's attention to their current situation.

"I don't deserve this kind of treatment. I'm not a criminal. I demand these handcuffs be taken off me, too." The trespasser tossed his head toward T.J. "He chased me. Tackled me. I'm the victim here."

"What were you doing here?" A steel thread ran through her friend's voice. "Or if you can't answer that question, maybe you can manage telling me who you are?"

The guy drew himself up even taller. "I'm a reporter for the *Texas Inquirer News* and was here to interview the Zimmermans."

"At ten o'clock at night?" Chloe asked, all three men turning their attention to her.

The prowler shrugged. "The lights were on, so I thought they were up."

Chloe folded her arms over her chest, trying to ignore T.J.'s gaze on her, which she was finding was next to impossible. "So you decided to go around to the back of the house and knock on the kitchen door? Is that your normal way to interview people? Perhaps you wanted to peep into windows to make sure people were up at this hour."

T.J. laughed and looked back at the intruder. "Who told you the Zimmermans were even here?"

The trespasser's forehead creased. "They aren't? My source sounded like they knew."

"They? More than one?" T.J. moved to the bottom of the stairs.

"Only one, but you aren't getting anything else from me, not even if male or female."

With blood streaked across his face, the reporter lifted his chin and glared at T.J.

"Who are you? Who is your source?" Rob asked, throwing a look to be quiet at Chloe and T.J.

"I'm Artie Franklin. I won't tell you my source. I don't have to. You'll find my credentials in my wallet in my back pocket."

Rob approached the man, removed his billfold and flipped it open. "Being a reporter doesn't give you free rein." He indicated to the officer nearby to take the man to the station, handing his patrol partner the wallet. "I'll be there soon." After the pair left with Artie Franklin, Rob climbed the stairs. "Let's finish this inside. It's freezing out here."

Chloe hadn't felt the cold because energy had been charging through her, the adrenaline only now beginning to subside. "I want to know who told him the Zimmermans were here."

"So do I." T.J. held the door open for Rob and Chloe, and then followed them into the house.

"I'll do my best to put pressure on him, but I've dealt with a few like this Artie Franklin. They will protect their sources at all costs."

Chloe swung around in the spacious foyer. "Give me a chance to talk to him. He might tell me. I didn't pound him into the ground and threaten him with a gun."

T.J. quirked a grin, then winced. "Hey, you wanted me to stop him. I did."

"The bottom line is that he found us when only a few knew the Zimmermans were staying here. We need to find out who leaked the info."

"It only takes one person saying something for it to get out. That's why in WitSec there are such strict protocols in place." T.J. looked her in the eye. "We're going to have to do the same thing."

She nodded. "We'll be moving from here, but I'll check in with you, Rob, to find out what you get from this Franklin character."

Rob frowned. "I don't like y'all being out of contact with me. I understand the Zimmermans have two more stops in the Dallas area. Will they be attending those?"

"I think they should cancel the tour, but it—"

"Yes, we'll be going to them." Paul interrupted Chloe. "We have people who are expecting to see us. We'll be attending both of those events. Mary and I have prayed about this and feel it's what we have to do."

Chloe spun around and faced the man. "Someone is after both of you. The wise thing to do is to put a stop to this tour."

Mary came up beside her husband. "That's why our publisher hired you and T.J. You'll protect us, but more important, the Lord will."

"Oh, great. Logic won't sway them," T.J. mumbled close to Chloe.

"Hush," she whispered, then faced the couple. "We're moving. That's the least we can do, since someone knows you two are here. Go pack. I want to be gone in half an hour."

As the Zimmermans mounted the stairs, Chloe shifted toward Rob. "I'll keep you informed, but we're going to have to be careful." She began walking her friend toward the door.

"Aren't you going to pack?"

"I never unpacked."

"I'm leaving him here." Rob waved toward the third officer standing in the entrance into the living room. "I'd feel better."

She opened the front door. "Fine. But he isn't to follow us. Okay?"

"I figured you'd say that. But you've got to promise me you'll call if there's more trouble."

"I will. You and I go back years." She watched him leave before turning toward T.J. "I may not have to pack, but it looks like you need to clean up. When we get to the new safe house, we need to decide which one of us is in charge. Both of us can't be. It isn't working." The best way to resist T.J.'s appeal was to concentrate on the job and keep everything professional. Or she would find herself falling in love again.

"Agreed." T.J. headed toward the rear part of the house.

Just before he disappeared down the hallway, a scream pierced the air.

FOUR

Chloe hit the stairs before T.J. and the police officer, but the pounding of their footsteps indicated they were right behind her as she rushed toward the Zimmermans' bedroom. Paul came out into the hallway, as pale as if he hadn't seen the light of day in months. He held in his hand a soft blue dress shredded to ribbons.

Chloe skidded to a halt in front of the man, dropping her hand with the gun to her side. "What happened?" She looked beyond and saw Mary sitting on the bed, trembling and hugging her arms to her chest.

"Someone…" Paul gulped, glancing at T.J. and Officer Bryant right behind her. "Someone did this. It wasn't like this—" he raised his hand, shaking the destroyed garment in

Chloe's face "—this morning. She wore it last night. She…" He opened and closed his mouth several times, then snapped it shut, clamping his lips together in a thin line.

"Officer, we'll take care of our clients. You should call Detective Matthews about this development. It's obvious someone was in the house sometime today."

T.J.'s calm voice floated to Chloe as she took Paul's arm and guided him back into the bedroom. She hadn't seen Mary this distraught even with all that had happened today. But cutting up one of her dresses was more personal.

Chloe sat next to Mary. "Where was your dress?"

"I brought two suitcases, and use one for putting my dirty clothes in. I—I thought I would do a load of laundry tomorrow since it was going to be one of our down days without an appearance." Mary dropped her head, scrubbing her hands down her face. "Sorry, I'm babbling," she finally said, lifting her gaze to Chloe.

"Was this dress in with the other dirty clothes? Was anything else cut up?" Chloe noticed T.J. standing at the entrance, scanning the room.

"Yes, it was with the other clothes. This was the only thing ruined. The dress is— was—my favorite one. Paul gave it to me on our last anniversary. Twenty blessed years. He picked it out himself. I even wore it to the event in Paris." Eyes glistening, Mary took a deep breath, then another, raising her quavering hand to comb her fingers through her hair. "I must look a mess. I…I…"

Chloe placed her arm around Mary. "You look fine. Why don't you let me pack the rest of your clothes? You can sit downstairs with Officer Bryant. When we wrap up everything here, we'll move to a new house. I don't want you to tell anyone—" she looked up at Paul, then back to Mary "—where you're staying."

"But my family needs to know." Mary blinked the tears from her eyes.

"I'll get you a number they can call. It's my employer's. She'll relay all messages to me.

Remember, do not tell anyone, even family, where you're staying," she repeated, not sure the couple fully understood the importance of keeping their location a secret.

"But this isn't my family's doing." Mary's voice quavered with each word.

"They might accidentally let something slip. It's very important. No one should know." Chloe stood.

Paul moved to the bed and sat on the other side of Mary, wrapping his arm around his wife. "How about the publicist for the publisher?"

"She can use the same number. We'll set up a network so your whereabouts can't be traced, but you'll still be able to stay in touch if you are needed." Chloe walked to T.J. "We'll give you a few minutes, but please don't touch anything in the closet until Detective Matthews gives his go-ahead."

T.J. stepped into the hallway. "Matthews should be here soon. I want him to dust for fingerprints and take Mary and Paul's to rule them out. Maybe we'll get something from that. But the question I want answered is how did the person get inside to destroy the dress? I know the alarm system isn't the best, but unless they knew the code, the alarm should have gone off."

"But as we talked about earlier, some systems can be circumvented if a person knows what he's doing. Were the windows wired?" Chloe asked. "I found two unlocked on the second floor when I did a walk-through earlier."

"No. Why didn't you say something?"

"Both weren't easily accessible and nothing seemed out of place. I thought maybe the owner left them unlocked. On the second floor, some people aren't as vigilant about locking them. Every closet and hiding place was checked, so no one was in the house after we came home."

"Which means they were here while we were away."

"Since the Zimmermans' schedule was public knowledge, that wouldn't be difficult to coordinate."

Footsteps coming up the stairs interrupted their conversation. Chloe glanced down the corridor as Rob and the police officer made their way toward them. Rob scowled, his long strides eating up the distance between them.

He stopped a few feet away from her. "What happened?"

"Someone cut up Mary's dress. It was in her suitcase with some other dirty clothes." Chloe observed the officer who moved around them and positioned himself at the bedroom door. Rob was taking this very seriously, which pleased her. Someone was toying with the Zimmermans. No one had been harmed—yet. But it was only a matter of time. She couldn't shake the feeling a lot more was to come. Ripping Mary's dress was personal. Had they known it was her favorite? "Just a sec." Chloe parted from the group and stepped back into the bedroom. "Paul, have you checked all of your clothes and belongings?"

"Not everything. Mary brought the suitcase out first and opened it on the bed—" Paul gestured toward the bag on the other side of the couple "—so I haven't had time to check. Should I now?"

"Wait until Detective Matthews talks with you two and gives the go-ahead. I want you both to make sure you have everything and your items and clothing are intact."

Rob entered, surveying the bedroom before bridging the distance to the Zimmermans. Chloe had intended to stay and listen, but T.J. clasped her hand and pulled her out into the hallway.

"I'd like to check the two windows that were unlocked. Also the ground below them."

"The first one is at the end of this hall." She pointed to the window on the side of the house that was well lit. "It's a straight drop with no trees or way to climb up to it unless a person uses a ladder."

"Maybe they did. A lot of people don't think anyone can get into their house through their second-story windows. They leave them unlocked and not wired to an alarm. That may be the case here. The Zimmermans arrived early this morning and didn't have a lot of time before they had to leave for the church. Where's the other window?"

"In the corner bedroom at the front of the house, which, if someone was using a ladder, wouldn't be their first choice."

T.J. walked to the first window at the end of the hall and examined it, without touching it, then checked out the second one nearby in the bedroom. "I'm assuming you didn't see anything unusual or you would have said something to me, but let's check outside. It rained yesterday, so the soil would be soft. If the intruder used a ladder, it would leave an indentation in the ground."

"I'll tell the officer where we're going and grab a flashlight."

When she went outside with T.J., they first checked the window facing the front of the house. An intruder would have to put the ladder on the driveway. "If he entered here, there's no way for us to tell."

"This wouldn't be the one. This entry is too obvious. They would check each window in the back of the place first." T.J. opened the gate and let Chloe go through ahead of him.

She stood under the window and inspected the ground around a bush directly under it. "This looks like someone put a ladder here."

"I'll have Matthews check for fingerprints here especially on the outside and the upstairs windowsill. You didn't touch that or the screen, which would have been removed to allow someone to climb inside, did you?"

"No, not other than the lock which I clicked shut."

T.J. made a full circle, taking in the surroundings. "That elm near the property blocks much of this side of the house from the next-door neighbor, but it wouldn't hurt for Matthews to talk to them in case they saw something like an unfamiliar car parked near here."

"Rob is thorough. Maybe he'll find evidence to help ID the person stalking the Zimmermans after he talks with them."

"Until then, let's get them moved to a safer house and let him do his job."

"Sounds like a good plan. None of us are going to get much sleep tonight, but tomorrow is a rest day and I figure we'll all need it." She headed for the front of the house. "Of course, that's only if no one discovers where we're going."

"This is a fortress," T.J. said and took a long sip of his coffee, relishing the jolt of caffeine. He turned from the window overlooking the large front yard of the new safe house, bathed in the morning sunlight.

Chloe closed the few feet between them. "And what's even better, no one knows about this place except the Zimmermans, you, me and Kyra. Paul and Mary are taking a nap. Paul was quite upset about his computer being wiped clean by the intruder. Apparently he and Mary have been working on another book in the series. It seems someone doesn't want them to write it. Fortunately, they have a backup."

"Going after a writer's computer is as personal as Mary's dress. Have we found out how anyone could know the significance of that piece of clothing?"

"Good question. I asked Mary about that. She opened the anniversary present at a party attended by a group of close friends. She made a big deal out of it because Paul actually went out and bought it. She called it her power dress. He usually has Mary's cousin who lives with them buy her gifts." She faced the window, side by side with T.J.

Her presence charged the air around him. Distracted a few seconds, he stared at her as she swallowed some of her drink. He pulled his attention away and continued his perusal of the yard, enclosed all the way around by an electrified six-foot fence. "I like that this is a much smaller house. Easier to defend."

"No one in our agency has used this yet. Kyra amazes me with her connections."

"Well, I'm in love with the security system. Everything is wired and will go off if someone tries to circumvent it."

Chloe chuckled. "Only someone in security would get excited about that."

"Or someone running for his life."

"The only thing we're missing is dogs patrolling the grounds."

"I guess we can't have everything." T.J. shifted toward her. "You wanted to talk about who should be the lead in this detail."

"Not anymore. The publisher contacted you about this job. You should be it."

He stuck his forefinger into his ear and wiggled it. "Did I hear correctly or has no sleep finally sent you over the edge?"

"Cute. I'm being practical. There needs to be one person in charge, and I wouldn't be here if you hadn't suggested it to Kyra. We can't debate tactics in the middle of a crisis. I trust you."

I trust you. Those words reverberated in his mind, leaving a warm feeling in their wake. He didn't trust. What had happened to him? His job certainly had taught him to be cautious, but he was even questioning the Lord. Was this innate distrust the reason he hadn't tried to stay in Chloe's life even after she didn't come to Washington? Had he been afraid in the end she would disappoint him, as so many people had in his line of work?

She grinned, two dimples showing. "Besides, if the publisher needs to talk to anyone about the security, that'll be your job."

"I've got big shoulders. I think I can handle it," T.J. said, forcing a laugh. He pushed his thoughts into the background. This wasn't the time to contemplate his trust issues.

"You'd better. That's the part of the job I don't like. Thankfully Kyra does that task."

"The publicist will be at the event tomorrow. I'll make sure she doesn't corner you."

"See, we're already working better together by talking about this."

A strand of her hair had come loose from her ponytail. T.J. clenched his hands tightly to keep from hooking it behind her ear. He moved toward the kitchen. "Do you want some more coffee?"

"No. I'm going to lie down while the Zimmermans are asleep, if that's okay with you. Then you can rest after me."

"I was going to suggest that very thing.

We both need some sleep, and although this place is a fortress, I think we should take turns guarding tonight, especially since there are only two bedrooms." As he entered the kitchen, he glanced back at her following him. "Okay?"

"Great. I feel so much better that we don't have a limousine service involved. Thanks for using your car to come here. It's been a *long* twenty-four hours since we started on this assignment." Chloe finished her coffee and put the cup in the sink. "I'd better snatch some sleep or I won't be able to keep my eyes open tonight."

"I know better. Kyra told me about one of your cases where you had to stay awake for over forty-eight hours and be alert until help got to you."

"I was younger then."

"Yeah, by a whole six months. That would make a big difference. See you in a couple of hours. Do you want me to wake you up?"

"No," she said quickly, her eyes widening slightly. "I always bring an alarm clock with me. I'll use that." She backed away. "See you in a few."

When she left, she seemed to take some of the energy with her. There was something vibrant about Chloe. He took his mug of strong coffee and walked through the small house, rechecking all points of entry before he stood at the large window in the living room and stared outside.

When the police officer had finally taken them to T.J.'s house to pick up his car early this morning before the sun was up, he'd grabbed an untraceable cell phone for communication with Kyra, Detective Matthews and the publisher. Then as he'd driven to this safe house, he and Chloe had kept an eye out for any car that might be following them. With less traffic at that time of day, it would have been easier to spy a familiar vehicle behind them.

And yet, beyond the six-foot chain-link fence, he sensed someone watching the place. Nothing concrete. Just a gut feeling.

Maybe that was his problem and the reason

he distrusted so easily. He was always looking over his shoulder, always scanning the crowd searching for someone who had evil intentions. He'd been taught to suspect everyone. He'd left the Secret Service and gone right into private protection. What was it like to have a normal life? To go to a nine-to-five job and come home—to a family. Would he ever do that with someone like Chloe?

Whoa. Where had that thought come from? Seeing Chloe again? He'd given up on having a family years ago when he was so often on the road with his job after his relationship with Chloe ended. He was still doing the same type of job—still gone from home a lot—which made him realize he needed to press Kyra about taking on a partner. Maybe then he could consider a life outside his job if he didn't travel much.

The next morning after showering and getting dressed, Chloe came into the kitchen for her first cup of coffee. The scent of it brewing drew her to the room. "Good morning. Did you two sleep all right?" she asked Mary and Paul. She'd slept soundly for four hours. She'd known T.J. stood guard and trusted him. That was a good feeling.

Scrambling eggs at the stove, Mary glanced over her shoulder. "Like a baby. I knew there was a reason we planned a couple of rest days in our month-long speaking tour. After all that has happened, I feel reenergized. How about you?"

"I slept as well as I usually do on the job." She was thankful she could operate on little sleep for short periods of time and still perform as she should.

"I hope you're hungry. I love to cook, but I don't get to as much as I used to. I thought we would have a big breakfast before we left. We have a long day ahead of us." Mary turned back to stir the eggs.

"Where's T.J.?" Chloe crossed the kitchen and filled a mug with coffee.

"He's in our bedroom, looking for bugs," Mary said.

"Bugs?"

"Listening devices." Paul buttered the toast after it popped up from the toaster.

"Be back in a sec." As Chloe moved through the six-room house, she scanned her surroundings, checking outside as she passed a window. When she arrived at the entrance to the bedroom the Zimmermans were using, she leaned against the doorjamb, took a sip of her coffee and asked, "Do you suspect there is a bug in their belongings?"

T.J. shrugged while running his bug sweeper over the couple's room. "Just a gut feeling we're being watched. I can't shake it. But if that's the case, how did they find us?"

"How did you get that?" Chloe gestured toward a black rectangular box on the end of a long, black pole.

"Kyra brought it to me first thing this morning. I think I woke her up."

"Why didn't you get me up?"

"Because it was your turn to sleep and you needed to. I'll wake you when we have a problem. Kyra talked to Matthews about the case late last night. It seems she knows him, too."

"Yeah, years ago they worked together on the police force. He's one of the reasons I went to work for her. What did she tell you?"

He walked toward her. "What prints they gathered were either Mary's, Paul's or an unknown person's."

"Were there any on the outside windowsill or the pane?"

"Surprisingly, those areas were clean of any prints."

"Like they had been wiped off?"

"Exactly. At least that's what Matthews thinks, or else gloves were used."

"Or they didn't use the window. There generally won't be prints on an upstairs outside windowsill that has a screen."

"That still is the most likely way they got in and out. The alarm wasn't set off or tampered with, so the intruder didn't come through the door unless he knew the code."

As he moved through the doorway, his arm brushed against hers. She caught a whiff of his lime aftershave. Her heartbeat revved for a few seconds. She stepped away while T.J. crossed the hall to the bedroom she'd slept in.

"I've already checked my bag. Yours is the last one. Oh, by the way, I'm having Kyra call the limo company and check for a GPS tracker on the one we used. It would be nice to find out if that was the way they discovered where the Zimmermans were staying."

"The limo company the Zimmermans were using wasn't public knowledge."

"But certain people knew—like the publicist who set it up."

"Why would the publicist do this?" Chloe tensed as he approached her suitcase on the floor on the other side of the bed.

T.J. ran the bug sweeper over her belongings, but it didn't sound. "That's it. Nothing on any of the items we brought from the other house. But I still feel something isn't right."

"Maybe you're being overzealous. Of course, I'd rather you be that than the opposite."

He strode into the hallway, inhaling a deep breath. "I'm sure glad Mary likes to cook."

"So am I, since I don't do much but the basics. Cooking for one doesn't inspire me to learn more."

"I feel the same way. Living in hotels will do that to you." T.J. waited for Chloe to go into the kitchen first.

Paul sat at the table while Mary carried the platter of scrambled eggs and bacon and put it in the center next to the stacked pieces of toast and the coffeepot.

"Good timing. Did you find anything?"

T.J. eased into the chair across from Paul while Mary and Chloe took a seat. "Nothing. That means most likely the person who came into the house two days ago was only there to wipe your computer and damage Mary's dress."

"But at least he doesn't know where we are now. That's a good thing." Mary spread her napkin in her lap.

"Yes," Chloe said, although a person could look at it from a different angle. If breaking and entering to plant a bug was the object, then the motive didn't seem as personal. It became much more personal if an intruder risked capture to taunt the couple with how easy it was for him to get to them. That meant the person was playing with them.

"Let's pray. I've worked up an appetite." Paul bowed his head and blessed the food, then began passing the platters around the table.

As Chloe handed T.J. the eggs and bacon, their gazes connected. In his dark eyes, full of concern, she could see he'd been thinking the same thing. Instead of being relieved he'd found no tracking devices, his expression reflected apprehension, his mouth tightening in a frown. No tracking device meant someone close had leaked the whereabouts of the Zimmermans. This could be another long day.

In the large auditorium, Paul wrapped up their appearance to a standing ovation. T.J. kept scanning the crowd, larger than the one at the church two days before. The place was packed. A detail of police was stationed around the room. Paul, dressed in his usual gray suit, had removed his coat early in their presentation and laid it over a chair behind him. He turned and shrugged into it, then straightened the red rosebud pinned to his lapel.

"Ready?" T.J. asked his client.

"Just a moment." Paul moved forward to meet some of the audience who had approached the stage.

He and Mary shook people's hands as they had before the presentation.

Chloe paused next to T.J. right behind the couple. "If only we could get them to come, speak and immediately leave," she whispered close to his ear, with her attention focused on the throng in the auditorium. She left him to watch the smaller group near the Zimmermans.

From the moment they had driven to the large school auditorium, he and Chloe had fallen into a rhythm where she often knew what needed to be done without him saying anything. She was making it easy to work with her. She was experienced, controlled and totally professional. He appreciated and admired her for that.

When Nancy Carson, the publicist for the publisher, walked out onto the stage and signaled for the Zimmermans to accompany her, Paul and Mary disengaged from the crowd after saying a prayer for the group.

"That's what I love about them. They're always thinking of others even with all the trouble they've been having." Chloe fell into step behind the couple while T.J. took the lead and went through the double doors first. The corridor was clear except for a half a dozen individuals, rendering the situation manageable.

As Paul and Mary walked side by side toward a room where a book signing was set up, T.J. took Paul's left and Chloe Mary's right. The publicists hurried before them, and when the Zimmermans stepped through the entrance, T.J. understood why. A television reporter with her camera was there, along with hundreds of people waiting for the couple.

Why weren't they told about this? This made a difference in how they controlled a room.

T.J. hadn't fully realized the scope of their popularity until today. Before Nancy could draw Paul and Mary to be interviewed by the young woman from a TV station in Dallas, the crowd pressed toward the Zimmermans. Someone knocked into T.J. He swiveled around to face an older gentleman, maybe seventy years old.

"Sorry. Someone pushed me from behind," the man said, but still jostled for a chance to speak to Paul.

T.J. glanced at Chloe being squashed against Mary. Why in the world had he thought this was manageable? Nothing about it was.

"Step back, please," T.J. shouted to the throng. When no one responded and kept pushing forward, he stuck his fingers into mouth and whistled, loud enough that the people around him backed away.

"Please move back and give the Zimmermans a chance to get to their table so they can sign your books." Chloe's clear, authoritative voice sounded above the murmurs.

The crowd parted and allowed them to escort Paul and Mary toward the area set up for the book signing. T.J. noticed Nancy beaming and the cameraman capturing the frenzy on tape.

After the couple had settled behind the table with a barrier between them and the crowd, T.J. still didn't let down his guard. The way the publicist was looking victorious, he wondered if she had set up that little scene when they had come into the room. Standing behind and to the side of Paul, T.J. looked toward Chloe, his tension reflected in her features.

"I hope we don't repeat that little scene at any other stops. Nothing happened today, but the person after them could cause some havoc. Perfect time to," she murmured, while her gaze swept the winding line that filled the large room.

"We'll make sure more police are in attendance next time they sign books and make sure with Nancy Carson there are no surprises like today with the television reporter." T.J. threw her a quick, assessing look. "You okay? I saw you getting pushed around."

"Besides my foot being stepped on, I'll survive. We might as well settle in here. This is going to take a few hours."

T.J. looked from one side of the room to the other. "Yep. At least."

By the end of the book signing, T.J. and Chloe hadn't left their positions for a couple of hours.

Tension vibrated the air, his every muscle taut and his nerves on edge as he waited for something to go wrong. He slanted a look at Chloe, her posture ramrod straight. At least their job was getting easier as the crowd finally thinned and the reporter got her story and left.

T.J. returned his focus on the large man pausing in front of Paul. The guy smiled at Paul and requested the book signed to him and his wife. Most of the people remaining were those who had sponsored the speaking engagement. Paul slid the book toward Mary to add her signature, then she passed it to the large gentleman. The couple had a good system down, but they had been autographing hundreds of books for almost two hours nonstop. T.J. didn't know how they did it.

The publicist bent over and checked the last box, then rose and said, "Sorry, everyone. These half a dozen are the last books." Nancy Carson waved at the short stack between Paul and Mary on the table. "I have a sheet where you can write down your address, and we'll send you a signed copy."

A few in line grumbled, but most hurried to Nancy Carson to sign up.

After autographing the last book, Mary rose. "If you'll excuse me, I'll be right back."

While Chloe went with her, Nancy stepped over to Paul. "This event was a huge success. At each stop more and more are attending and, even better, buying your books. I'm glad we've arranged a book signing at most of the rest of the stops on the tour. We've gotten good coverage."

A scowl descended over Paul's features. "Not the kind of coverage I want. I've been following what has been written. It seems the reporters are only focusing on the bad things happening."

"But that hasn't discouraged anyone from coming. Any publicity is better than none. This has gone national. I won't be surprised if you two sell tons of books over the next couple of weeks. *Take Back America* has risen to number one at all of the major on-line bookstores and is still on the *New York Times* bestsellers list. You two are spreading your message. That's what you wanted, as well as your publisher."

Paul shifted toward T.J. "I'm ready to go. It's been a long day."

Nancy started toward a bookstore employee as she addressed Paul. "A television station wants you to appear on their morning show the day after tomorrow before you head to your next town. I told them you two will be ecstatic."

Paul's frown deepened. "I would have appreciated you running it by my wife and me before agreeing. Squeezing in any more doesn't give us much time to regroup and rest."

"You can do that at the end of the tour." Nancy smiled and continued toward the employee.

"That woman only looks at Mary and me with dollar signs in her eyes," Paul said when Nancy was out of earshot.

"A television station is a safer place to protect you than a large crowd. Why don't you do more of that?" T.J. asked.

Paul's mouth twisted, then settled into a neutral expression. "Mary and I want to touch people personally. These speaking tours give us a better chance than being in front of a camera. I'm not a big fan of television anyway. Too many people are wrapped up in watching it rather than living the life they were meant to. They use it as a form of escape."

"The room is clearing out. Let's get Mary

and Chloe and leave. We need to meet Kyra Hunt to trade cars again."

"You really think someone would put a tracking device on the car in the parking lot?"

"Yes."

Paul shook his head. "How do you live distrusting everyone?"

"It's my job. If I wasn't so cautious, someone could be killed."

"Still, it has to affect you. I find it so much easier to trust the Lord. He'll prevail."

"In the meantime, I'm here to protect people who need it." But he couldn't argue it hadn't affected his personal life. When had he stopped trusting in God?

T.J. met Chloe and Mary returning from the restroom. "Ready?"

Chloe nodded. "I'll call Kyra to meet us."

"Stay inside by this door. I'll bring the car around." T.J. pushed out of the double doors leading to the side parking lot and jogged toward the rental car he'd exchanged with Kyra en route to the event. The still air cooled him, and he relished being outside after being stuffed in a room with so many people, all wanting the Zimmermans' attention. He should be used to that scene after the Secret Service.

T.J. slipped behind the steering wheel and drove toward the side of the building. When he pulled up near the double doors, Chloe rushed the couple to the rental. She sat in the back with Mary while Paul clambered into the front passenger seat.

Although T.J. would switch back to his gray Jeep Grand Cherokee before continuing to the safe house, he would have Kyra check the rental for a tracking device. Ten minutes later, he parked behind his car, which Kyra sat in. "I'll only be a sec. Stay in here until I give you the go ahead." He made his way to the Jeep's driver's side.

Kyra climbed out. "Everything go okay?"

"So far so good, but I won't breathe easy until we're at the safe house. Before you turn in this rental, see if anyone attached a tracking device. We'll follow the same procedure with a new rental car tomorrow. At least that way I'll know we aren't being tracked."

"I will, and I checked your Jeep. It was clean. Not that I was expecting to find anything. But I like to take every precaution possible." Kyra exchanged keys with T.J. "Drives my husband crazy at times."

"Tell Michael hi, and congratulations on another baby."

The owner of Guardians, Inc., smiled. "I will, and when this is over, I hope you'll come to dinner. I want to discuss your proposal to become my partner. With another baby arriving in five months, I need to stay home more."

T.J. walked toward the rental with Kyra. "Great." At the car he opened the front passenger door. "Let's go."

As Mary and Paul exited the rental, T.J. introduced them to Kyra.

"I wish we weren't meeting under these circumstances. I'm a fan of yours." Kyra shook hands and then hugged Chloe. "You'll be just fine with T.J. and Chloe."

T.J. escorted Paul to his Jeep. Although on a residential street Kyra had picked at random, he was still alert for anything unusual. When a blue van turned the corner and headed toward them, he hurried his pace and quickly ushered Paul into the front seat while Chloe helped Mary into the back. The van picked up speed, the driver rolling down his window.

FIVE

As the blue van grew nearer to the Jeep, Chloe said, "Get down." With her hand on her gun, she stood in front of the back window to block Mary.

T.J. followed suit. Tension poured off him as the van came to a stop and the driver leaned out his window. "Do you know where 1245 South Fourth Street is? My GPS sent me here, but this isn't Fourth."

"Sorry. I can't help you."

"Oh, okay." The driver moved his van slowly forward ten yards and asked Kyra, who had positioned herself by the rental.

"There isn't a Fourth Street around here, but there is a Forest. That sort of sounds like the one you're looking for. Could there be a mix-up?" Kyra asked while waving T.J. on.

Chloe climbed in T.J.'s Jeep and kept her eye on Kyra and the van driver as T.J. pulled away. When T.J. rounded the corner, she said, "You all can get up now."

Paul glanced back. "What's going on? The guy was only looking for an address."

"We don't know what his real intentions were, so we prepare for the worst. If we don't, we could be caught off guard." T.J. made another turn, then quickly a third one.

"How sad you have to suspect everyone. I couldn't do your job."

Mary's words stayed with Chloe the whole way to the safe house. For a good part of her life as a law enforcement officer and then a bodyguard, she'd had to be tough and strong for others around her. Even as a teen with her father gone a lot, she'd had to be there for her mother, but she had dreamed of having her own family and doing things differently from her mom. Somewhere along the line, that dream had gotten pushed to the background. Was it because she couldn't quite forget those times her mother had cried, lamenting how much she and her husband had been in love?

But seeing Kyra's pregnancy starting to show had revived Chloe's yearning to be a wife and mother. At first, when dating Adam, she'd thought he would be the one, but she must have instinctively known he wasn't suited for her because she hadn't been totally able to commit to him. He'd ended up dating another woman behind her back.

After T.J. and Adam, she wasn't sure having a family was in God's plan for her. If she couldn't make a total commitment, a marriage wouldn't work. She'd seen that firsthand with her parents.

Later that night, Chloe entered the living room and found T.J. staring out the front window. He threw a look over his shoulder at her, then went back to studying the landscape outside. "Do you see anything suspicious?" She planted herself next to him and gazed into the darkness.

"No, but Kyra called. She found a tracking

device on the rental by the rear left tire. She's working with a sketch artist to draw a picture of what the man in the blue van looked like. The police will have it with them tomorrow at the last speaking engagement in Dallas."

"Good. I know you took down the license number. Have they tracked the owner?" She found herself narrowing her eyes, trying to see into the blackness.

"Yes, and as you guessed, it was stolen and found abandoned about ten blocks away."

"Any fingerprints?"

"Tons, but none on the steering wheel or the driver's door."

"With a picture of the guy, they can run a facial recognition program for a match."

"True—maybe we'll get a break and he'll be in the system."

T.J. shifted toward her, his eyes shielded by the shadows.

But Chloe felt them pierce through her as though he were assessing her and trying to figure something out. "I guess we scared him away since there were three of us, ready to draw our guns."

"Plus we were blocking Paul and Mary from his view. Before he got a second shot off, he'd have been dead." He narrowed the space between them and grasped her hand. "But we came close today. One of us could have been shot."

The feel of his hand around hers sent her heartbeat racing. Memories of their past deluged her. If her mother hadn't been sick with cancer, would she have gone with T.J. to Washington? She'd asked herself that many times over the years. But when her mother had recovered, she still hadn't been able to shake her doubts about T.J.'s true feelings, or she would have moved to Washington. Even though she'd ended up comparing all men she dated to T.J.

"And we know he doesn't care if others get hurt while he's hunting the Zimmermans." She barely strung the words together to form a coherent sentence, but T.J. was waiting for her to say something.

"Right. He gave the Zimmermans' driver in Dallas a concussion, and that little stunt in Paris injured a few spectators. Thankfully not bad, but still, the potential was there." He shrank the space between them even more. "I do know one thing. I didn't want anything to happen to you today."

Her mouth went dry, and she swallowed several times. "You don't need to worry about me. I can take care of myself. I've been doing it for years."

"I know. But that doesn't mean I don't want you to be careful."

"What are you doing, T.J.?"

"Telling you I care about you." He ran his free hand through her loose curls.

Her pulse throbbed. "We didn't work in the past."

For a long moment, he searched her face as though probing for some insight into what she was thinking. He released his hold on her and stepped back. "You're right. I don't want anyone to get hurt, whether it is the client, a spectator or my partner," he said in a professional voice, erasing the past few minutes as if they hadn't occurred.

Disappointment flitted down her length. What was going on between T.J. and her? Had what she'd felt the past few moments been her imagination? "I agree."

Tall, his posture straight, almost rigid, he stared outside again, his hands stuffed into his pockets. She studied his hard profile, part of it in the dark, and wished she could read his thoughts. He could still affect her, even when she steeled herself against his charms.

"Have you ever wondered what would have happened to us if you had gone to Washington?" he said, finally breaking the silence.

"Have you wondered what would have happened to us if you had turned down the job to guard the vice president and stayed in Dallas?"

He dipped his head. "Touché. And to answer your question, yes, I have thought about it."

Her eyes grew round. "What?"

"It wouldn't have worked out. You needed

to stay and take care of your mother. If you hadn't, you would have been resentful that I took you away. And if I had turned down the position, I would have become resentful, wondering what opportunities I had passed over because I didn't take the job. We were both young and trying to find a place in our field. We weren't ready for that kind of commitment."

Are we now? Will you ever be ready to let go of our distrust and fear? She wanted to ask that question, but bit the inside of her cheek to keep the words inside her. "You left the Secret Service early. Do you regret being an agent?"

He swung around with several feet still between them. "Yes and no."

She waited for him to elaborate, but when he didn't, she examined the planes of his jaw line. "That's a complete answer?"

"Let me ask you if you regretted being a Dallas police officer. I thought you would make a career out of being one, but you only remained one five years after I left."

"I stayed because of my mother. After Dad died, she moved from Houston to Dallas because she needed her family and I was it. I think she knew something was wrong with her. Not long after she came, she got sick."

"Yeah, I remembered when we started dating she'd just moved to Dallas and was staying with you."

"I'm glad I had that time with her. If I hadn't, I would have regretted it. I was the only family Mom could turn to."

"Why did you quit the force? You were good at what you did. I could see you moving up the ranks quickly."

"I made detective and was excited that I could work on homicides. My mother had passed away from a reoccurrence of her cancer about six months before that and I thought a change was what I needed. Day in and day out was too much for me." For a moment, surprise gripped her. She'd never given an indication that too much death was taking the life out of her. "I left because I needed more in a job than it could provide. How about you?"

"Yes." He paused, as though trying to compose what he said next. "It was pretty much that for me, too."

His evasive tone indicated he was holding something back. Her curiosity piqued, she wanted to ask him what, but instead said, "Not being a human shield? Isn't that what we're doing?"

"Yes, but we have a say in who we protect and more control over the situation. With that said, I have something I need to tell you."

She tensed. "This doesn't sound good. What's wrong?"

"I've proposed to Kyra to buy into Guardians, Inc. Today she expressed interest. I believe she'll take me up on my proposition. She wants more time at home, especially since the new baby is coming soon."

"Why are you telling me this?"

"Because you work there. I don't want you to feel uncomfortable about the situation."

"And if I was?" She held her breath waiting for his answer because this was her job—a good one with an added bonus she felt she was helping people in need.

"Then I would look for something else. I'm not tied to Dallas. I have connections in other cities."

The thought that he would move away again if she said she was uncomfortable bothered her. Why wouldn't he fight for her? Change her mind? She'd known Kyra was pulling back from the agency, that her family was demanding more of her time. Her taking on a partner wasn't a surprise but a logical step for her employer. But that would mean T.J. would be her boss. How did she feel about that? Maybe it was time to make a change, possibly even in her job. She'd been thinking more about that lately.

"Chloe?"

There was a wealth of inquiry in that one word. Seeing him again, being around him, she had begun to realize what kind of relationship they could have after the assignment was over. Could they return to the way it had been in the past? She needed to say something to him, but… "I don't have an answer for you. We have history. Although I know you wouldn't intend for it to stand between us, it might."

"Fair enough. This may be a moot point. I don't have a definite answer from Kyra. We'll talk about it when we finish protecting Paul and Mary. I told you now because I didn't want any secrets between us. Not that my interest in Guardians, Inc., is a secret, just not public knowledge." His mouth curved into a smile.

"Good partners are honest with each other."

"Agreed, and that's why I appreciate your honest opinion about the situation."

In that moment, something shifted in this new relationship between her and T.J. In the past, she'd never felt totally on equal footing with him. He'd been her team leader on a big counterfeit case she'd worked on as an undercover operative. Even when they'd started dating, always in the back of her mind had been the fact he was older and a more experienced law enforcement officer. She hadn't been a rookie, but close enough.

For the first time she felt on equal footing—what would happen if he became her boss?

"Over the years I've learned to stand up for myself and give my opinion. I've changed." Nine years ago she hadn't been fully honest until the end of their relationship when she'd refused to go to Washington and stayed to help her mother.

"I've noticed. I've changed, too. More mellow."

"Mellow? Not from where I am," she said with a chuckle. "You rushed right out the door to catch the intruder a couple of nights ago."

His laugh filled the air. "You aren't going to let me forget that. You got the better end of that deal."

"Yes, and *now* I'm grateful for that. But at the time I wanted to clobber you." She tried to force the tight muscles in her neck and shoulders to relax, but it wasn't working.

"That's okay. I got clobbered by Artie Franklin. And speaking of that reporter, Kyra said he's still remaining quiet about his informant. She's going to dig into his life and see what she finds."

"If anyone can get him to talk, it will be Kyra. Anything else?" *What really made you quit the Secret Service?*

"Nothing really. Matthews can't find the car that was parked next to the limo at the church. The driver is fully recovered, but can't give us any more information. Kyra is checking into his past, too, to make sure he wasn't in on it."

"Could he be the leak to the reporter?" Weariness blanketed Chloe, and she turned to lean against the windowsill.

"Kyra mentioned that. It's possible, but for some reason doesn't feel right to me. You should get some rest. I'll take the first watch tonight."

"Are you sure?"

He moved closer and put his hands on her

shoulders. "Definitely. You're wound tight. I can feel the knots."

"I get like this during an assignment. All my stress ends up on my shoulders."

"Turn around. Let me see what I can do."

When she did as he said, his fingers kneaded the base of her neck and along her shoulders, working to ease the tension. Bit by bit it fell away. "You're hired. No matter what I do, I always feel this tense after a few days on a job. I've tried putting heat there, but your massage is much better."

"It's because those knots have to be broken up."

A sigh slipped from her lips. "When did you get so good?"

"This can be pretty common in our line of work. Our stress has to go somewhere."

"Where does yours go?"

"Into sleepless nights."

Finally, she swung around, needing to put some space between them. "I think I got the better deal. I need my sleep, which is my cue to leave and get some before it's my turn to stand guard. Thanks."

"Good night, Chloe. See you in four hours."

She left T.J. standing at the window, staring out front again. At the doorway, she looked back at him, rubbing her hand over her neck and shoulder. The deep ache had vanished, but not the questions their conversation had raised. They both had changed in nine years. He wasn't the same man she had fallen in love with once, and she wasn't the same woman. That should be reason enough to guard against his appeal.

Standing backstage at a downtown hotel with a theater-style auditorium, Chloe watched the throng filling up the large area—a sea of red chairs with almost two thousand people in them. Rob Matthews was in the dressing room waiting with Mary and Paul for the crowd to be seated. At least the couple had agreed to come early and not to use the main entrance into the building after hearing that the driver in the blue van hadn't been legit and the rental had had a GPS tracker attached to it.

All the uniformed police watching the auditorium, double the number after yesterday, had a drawing of the driver, which Chloe thought looked remarkably like the man she'd seen.

She studied the audience as they filed into the massive room through the main sets of doors in the back while T.J. positioned himself on the other side and observed the individuals coming through the right entrance. Rob thought it would be better if they scanned the crowd while he stayed with the couple because they had seen the driver yesterday.

As much as she wished she saw the perpetrator in the auditorium, not one person looked similar. That didn't mean he wasn't here somewhere, disguised. The sheer numbers entering made it impossible to be sure he wasn't among them. And no amount of trying to persuade the Zimmermans to cancel had worked.

The lights dimmed two minutes before

Mary and Paul were expected on stage. The people, most still standing, moved to their seats. Mary and Paul would speak for an hour, then sign books at the table set up for them in the lobby. A copy of their most recent book had been included as part of the ticket sale. Probably not everyone would want an autograph, but enough would that it would be hours before they left for the security of the safe house. Then they would repeat it all in San Antonio, their next stop.

Paul joined T.J. while Rob escorted Mary to Chloe's side of the stage. The lights came back up and the couple strolled onto the stage with Chloe and T.J. closely behind them. A story had run on the news the day before about the fact the Zimmermans had two bodyguards because of threats made against them, and still the whole auditorium was crammed with people eager to hear their message, to fight for their families, their communities, to stand up to gangs and criminals who wanted to defy them.

As before, Chloe took the right side while

T.J. canvassed the left side. The bright lights shining in their faces made the task difficult. Paul began speaking, then Mary. Throughout their talk the audience erupted into applause at different points.

"This is our country. We'd better determine what is acceptable and not let just the vocal people determine it. The silent majority has a responsibility not to be silent any longer," Paul said about halfway through the talk.

The people rose, cheering, the sound deafening. Chloe tensed. This would be a good time to make a move. But within minutes the crowd took their seats and silence ruled as Mary spoke.

A woman in the back of the front section screamed. Red smoke billowed into the air from the center section while from behind the curtains smoke flooded the stage as the audience surged to their feet, yelling. Chloe grabbed Mary's arm while T.J. took Paul's. The people from behind the stage poured out of there, running away with the fleeing crowd as red smoke rolled and swelled from the back, too.

Chloe started for the steps when she caught sight of Rob carrying a woman from behind the curtain. Her long curly dark hair flowed over the detective's arm, her face turned toward his chest.

"There's another one down near the dressing rooms. I think these are smoke bombs, but we need to get out of here in case there's something else coming," Rob shouted.

T.J. looked at Chloe.

"Go. Rob's here," Chloe said, moving between Paul and Mary on the far right by the stairs leading to the theater floor.

Paul wrenched away from Chloe's grasp. "I'm going with T.J. There may be more hurt backstage. Please make sure that Mary gets out all right."

"No, Paul. I'll stay and help, too."

He swung around and took hold of Mary. "Get out of here." Then he hurried after T.J.

Chloe started after him, but Rob blocked

her passage. "You and Mary need to leave with me. I'll get some help back here."

"I can't leave. What if…" Mary's eyes glistened.

Reddish-gray smoke continued to roll across the stage like dense fog, its stench spreading. Chloe tightened her hold on her client. "T.J. will take care of Paul. Let's go."

Mary didn't resist, but kept looking back while Chloe focused on a way out of the theater—the nearest exit was a third of the way to the back of the theater. She kept Mary close to her. All around Chloe, the mob tried cramming through the few exits—two sets on the sides and another two in the back, six double doors with two thousand individuals hurrying to leave.

Mary gasped and all color drained from her face. Chloe glanced back. Flames licked up the curtains on the left side of the stage—where T.J. and Paul had disappeared.

SIX

T.J. turned and saw the burning curtain fall onto the stage and the blaze engulf the material. Flames ran across the stage, completely cutting them off from getting out of the theater from that direction. That left only one other—the backstage door, which felt like riding into an ambush.

"We'll check the dressing room area. Start praying that the back door isn't blocked." Coughing, T.J. used the crook of his elbow to cover his nose and mouth, his eyes stinging.

Paul did likewise, staying right at his side as T.J. plunged into the smoky air. Up ahead through the haze, he saw a figure lying on the floor. T.J. increased his pace, and when he reached the prone body, he knelt and felt for a pulse. With coughs racking his body, Paul squatted next to T.J.

"He's alive. Help me get him up and we'll drag him between us." T.J. hoisted the obese man up by the left side while Paul took the right.

"Why isn't the sprinkler system working?" Paul shouted over the crackling noise of the fire.

"Good question." Sweat rolling down his face, T.J. started again for the back of the theater. With a look over his shoulder, he spied the fire moving away from him but toward the audience—and Chloe and Mary.

At the door, T.J. slammed his hand down on the bar to open it. Nothing happened. The lever didn't budge. Locked?

Someone in front of Chloe went down, tripping over another person who'd fallen. With Rob carrying the unconscious woman, Chloe and Mary were left to grab the two on the floor and pull them up before the stragglers behind them ran them over. One man leaped over Chloe, barely missing her and the young lady she was helping. An older gentleman plowed into Mary and sent her flying into the teenage girl trying to get up with her assistance. They both went down again. Chloe managed to haul the woman to her feet before she turned her attention to her client and the teen.

All the while heat, smoke and flames headed their way faster than the people could move through the exits. She would be a fool not to be afraid, but she didn't have time to give in to her fear. She could when she got Mary outside.

The sound of something crashing onto the stage spurred the mob to hurry even more. The pounding of her heartbeat thundered against Chloe's skull. Smoke from the fire reached outward, engulfing the whole theater.

"Let's put him down and both of us try to open the door. It's not locked. It seems like something is blocking it," T.J. said right before a ceiling beam ten yards away from them collapsed onto the stage. "No wonder everyone fled out of the stage area."

Coughing, Paul dropped the man, who slid down, almost taking T.J. with him. He released his hold before they were a tangled mess on the floor.

Facing Paul, T.J. said, "One, two, three."

Both slammed their shoulders into the metal door. It inched open.

Again T.J. and Paul struck it. Fresh air blew in from the small gap and fueled T.J.'s determination to budge whatever was on the other side—but also fed the fire with oxygen.

The third attempt moved the obstruction enough that T.J. squeezed his shoulder through the space and poked his head outside. The big Dumpster had been dragged in front of the door. The stench of garbage mixed with the smell of smoke. The wail of sirens echoed down the alley. Police and a couple of firefighters charged toward them.

Relieved, T.J. ducked back in, staying next to Paul low to the ground. "Help is coming." When he heard the Dumpster being moved, he said, "Let's get this guy up, so when the door can open all the way, we can get him out into the fresh air."

As Paul helped him hoist the huge man up, he looked at T.J. over the top of the victim's head. "We'll be all right, but what about Mary and Chloe?"

T.J. stared at the wall of fire edging its way toward them, seeking the fresh air. "They're fine," he said and prayed to the Lord he was right. *Chloe and Mary are in Your hands.* He didn't know what he would do if something happened to Chloe—or Mary.

Screams erupted around Chloe as the fire danced along the front of the stage and up the walls toward the back. Panic mushroomed as the fire exploded nearby.

"Get behind me," Rob said to Chloe and Mary.

"Lord, put a shield of protection around these people," Mary said as she looked around.

"Amen." Chloe had seen this kind of crowd

chaos before. From what she'd read about the stink bombs in Paris, that was mild compared to this.

A man near Chloe pulled another guy back and surged into his place. The first man returned and jumped on him. In the midst of the mob, a fight broke out. The sight shot adrenaline through Chloe, and her heartbeat accelerated even more. People circled past the two wrestling on the floor and kept heading for the exit. Sweeping her gaze through the theater, Chloe glimpsed the same thing happened at all the doors—panic taking over.

Chloe grasped Mary and pulled her even closer. With Rob in front, Chloe covered the area behind them and to the sides.

Finally the double doors loomed a few yards ahead.

"We're almost out of here," Chloe said close to Mary's ear as the noise around them kept rising.

Tears running down her face, Mary nodded, then started coughing.

Gray smoke like a menacing veil mingled with what red was left in the air above them, becoming thicker—darker.

Rob, carrying the passed-out woman, burst through the exit, followed by Mary and Chloe. The mob dispersed out into the lobby, charging for the bank of glass doors that led outside. Fire trucks lined the front of the building while firefighters and police swarmed the area inside, helping the crowd to move in a safe manner. Some of the firefighters were pushing into the auditorium against the tide of people.

Out in the fresh air Chloe propelled Mary farther from the theater. Police waved the throng past the barricades set up. Rob sought paramedics for the woman. As Chloe scanned the crowd for the perpetrator, she searched for T.J. and Paul, too.

Were they still in the theater behind the stage where the fire had started? She *needed* to see T.J. and Paul—that they were alive and safe.

* * *

The paramedic took the oxygen mask from T.J. "I'm okay," T.J. said. "How is the man we brought out?"

"He's being transported to the hospital, but he did recover consciousness."

"Praise God." Paul also gave his mask back. "Can we go now?"

"I'm fine with that, but the police officer wants to talk with you." The paramedic waved his hand toward a young woman waiting a few feet away.

She approached them when the EMT left. "What is your name and contact information?"

After T.J. told her, he asked, "Please see if you can contact Detective Rob Matthews. I'm a bodyguard hired to guard Paul Zimmerman here." T.J. indicated his client next to him. "I need to know if the detective and the women with him made it out okay." T.J. went on to explain why Matthews was involved.

The woman officer stepped away and spoke into the receiver at her shoulder.

Paul shifted from one foot to the other. "We should go around front and see if we can find Mary and Chloe. I need to know they're okay."

So do I, especially Chloe. She's here because of me. A vision of Chloe, concern deep in her eyes, as she'd left with Mary, taunted him.

"You think this area is a madhouse? The front will be twenty times worse as all the audience exits. I'm hoping she can track down Detective Matthews and he'll have Mary and Chloe with him." Safe. *Please, Lord. I haven't asked much lately. Please let them be unharmed.*

As T.J. waited for the officer to return, Chloe haunted his thoughts. Her smile could melt him, although he did his best not to let her know the effect it had on him. Her long, wavy hair down around her shoulders—the memory of letting it slip through his fingers. Her scent that teased him every time she came near him.

The policewoman retraced her steps to T.J.

and Paul. "Detective Matthews is on his way and he told me to tell you he would bring Mrs. Zimmerman and Chloe. You're not to go anywhere until he arrives. You two can sit in my patrol car. He asked me to stay with you."

Paul collapsed on the backseat behind the driver while T.J. slipped in next to him, his gaze intent on the direction Chloe and Mary would come from. Until he saw Chloe with his own eyes, he wouldn't be satisfied she was okay. He knew all the things that could happen in a crowd during a disaster. Pandemonium ruled, and that made it possible for the person hunting Mary to take her out. Chloe would protect her client, putting herself in harm's way. The realization iced his blood.

Coming around the side of the theater about a hundred yards from the building, Chloe glimpsed a woman officer standing next to a squad car. Through the windshield she noticed two figures in the back of it. "Is that them?" she asked Rob, who flanked Mary's other side as they weaved their way through the throng milling behind the barricades.

"I think so. I'm not personally familiar with Officer Parks."

As she swept her glance over the crowd, Chloe caught sight of the smoke churning from the roof of the theater. "What happened in there? We saw red smoke bombs first, then a real fire."

"The woman I carried outside came from the back area of the stage, where some of the red smoke was. Once she is tended to at the hospital, I plan to talk with her. Maybe she saw something, or maybe she's the one who set off the smoke bomb."

"Why would she do that? I don't know her. What have I done to her?" Mary stared straight ahead, a dazed expression on her face as though in overload.

Chloe couldn't blame her after all that had happened to Mary and Paul this week. She knew one thing. This tour could not continue. If need be, she would decline the assignment and hope T.J. would, too. Mary and Paul had no business being out in public until whoever was after them was caught. She'd never walked away from a job in the middle before, but she cared about Mary and Paul and wanted to keep them alive, so she would leave if that would keep Mary and Paul from continuing the book tour.

"What sets someone off can be one of a thousand reasons, big or small. Some you can't even comprehend. When dealing with situations like this you need to look at everyone as a suspect," Chloe finally answered.

"I agree, Mrs. Zimmerman. What Chloe says is true. If you want to stay alive, there's no question the person doing this wants you and your husband harmed. This isn't a prank like Paris." Rob stepped up to the officer and introduced himself. "Can you drive these folks to their house and stay there until I arrive?" Then he turned to Chloe. "I'm staying here and working this scene. We'll talk later."

"No. I don't want Officer Parks driving us. We can take care of it. The fewer people who know where we are the better."

Rob pulled her away from Mary and lowered his voice. "I can't force you, Chloe, but the Zimmermans are in danger."

"Why do you think T.J. and I were hired? But yesterday the guy after them put a tracker on the rental so he would know where they were staying. I need this evening to convince Mary and Paul to cancel their tour and retreat to a safe place. Maybe even stay where we are until you find whoever is doing this." The sound of the car door behind her opening and closing alerted her a few seconds before T.J. joined them.

"I suggest you quit the chitchatting and let's get out of here. The person responsible for this is probably somewhere in this crowd." T.J. gestured toward the theater where the firefighters were beginning to bring the blaze under control. "I called Kyra and told her what happened. She'll meet us to exchange cars again."

Chloe swung her attention to Rob. "Will it appease you if Officer Parks follows us to the exchange in our rental to make sure everything goes all right?"

Rob nodded. "But we're still talking tonight. I need your address, and I promise no one will track me. Where's your rental?"

T.J. pointed to a green Chevy not far away.

"I'll talk with Officer Parks, then walk with you to your car."

As Rob approached the police officer, T.J. escorted Paul to Chloe and Mary. Paul embraced his wife for a long moment. Chloe heard the words *I love you,* and turned away to give them some privacy while watching the people around them.

"Let's go," Rob said when he came back. As they walked toward the Chevy about a hundred yards across the parking lot, he continued. "Mr. and Mrs. Zimmerman, are you sure you can't think of anyone who would do something like this? There was a lot of anger behind what happened today. Four red smoke bombs were set off to cause panic much worse than the stink bombs at the Paris event. Then there was a fire, too."

Paul scowled. "Can a smoke bomb start a fire?"

"Not likely." Rob opened the back door for Mary. "A flash bomb would be more likely to do that."

Mary climbed into the rental. "Then why the smoke bombs if the person was setting a fire?"

"Don't know the answer, but I may know more when I talk with the fire investigator about how it started. That may be a while, though."

"Thank you, Detective." Mary leaned back against the seat and closed her eyes.

After shutting the door, Chloe faced Rob. "I echo her thanks. I hope you can give us some answers this evening." She gave her friend the address of the safe house. "Call when you arrive at the gate and I'll open it."

"Take care, Chloe. We're coming up empty with the clues we've found so far. I have my partner tracking down one lead from the photo of the man yesterday."

"Why didn't you tell me this right away?"

"I found out right before everything started and since then we've been kind of busy."

"Thanks for being here today." Chloe gave Rob a small smile.

T.J. shook Rob's hand. "See you later."

Her friend started back toward the theater, homing in on the fire captain in charge. Chloe expelled her breath slowly. "We have our work cut out for us. We need to convince the Zimmermans to cancel."

"They will. If not, I'll get the publisher to cancel it."

As T.J. slipped into the driver's seat, Chloe rounded the rental and slid into her position next to Mary.

Paul angled around and peered at his wife. "Before we go, I want to make it clear that Mary and I agree that the tour has to be canceled. We can't put people in danger, and today this person made it clear he didn't care who was in his way."

Thank You, Lord. Now we have a chance to protect Mary and Paul.

* * *

"We caught a break, or so we thought," Rob said when he entered the safe house later that evening.

T.J. closed the door behind the detective and turned toward him. "I like the first part of your sentence. You need to improve on the last bit, though."

"I wish I could." Rob surveyed the entry hall. "Where's everyone? I want to say this only one time. I need to return to the station as soon as possible."

"Chloe, Paul and Mary are in the kitchen cleaning up the dinner dishes. I volunteered to be on door duty."

"I wish I could do that at home. My wife won't take any excuse. All the duties are split fifty-fifty, and I can't really say anything since she works as much as I do."

T.J. started for the back of the house. "More than a detective in a big city?"

"Yep. She's a doctor in the E.R. Since we don't have children, she fills in when needed, if possible."

"It sounds like you have an understanding wife."

"Yes. It was a great day when I met her."

T.J. listened to the love in Matthews's voice, and he was bothered by the fact he didn't have what the detective had. For a long time, he hadn't even considered having a wife and family. Then he'd met Chloe and that had changed. He'd started thinking about the possibility of getting married. But on one occasion when they had dated, she'd expressed how she hoped to have children one day, and he hadn't seen that in his future as a Secret Service agent. Was that one of the reasons he'd jumped at the chance to go to Washington D.C. and be on the vice president's detail? He'd never thought he had a commitment phobia. Did he? Or had the timing been all wrong? And even if it had been, that didn't mean it was right now.

When they entered the kitchen, Chloe looked at Rob. "Do you know how the fire started?"

"Not yet, but by morning the rubble should

have cooled enough for the arson investigator to go through it. I have a few things to ask and tell you."

Mary crossed the room. "Then let's sit down in the living room. I'm exhausted. I'm sure you'll want me to be fully awake, but I can't stand much longer."

Paul took her hand and accompanied his wife out of the kitchen.

T.J. liked the way Paul and Mary supported each other. There were times he'd needed that but hadn't experienced it. He settled on the couch across from Paul, Mary and Chloe.

Matthews stood at the end of the coffee table, his mouth set in a grim line. "There were sixteen people who went to the E.R. Five of them were hospitalized."

Stiff, Mary blinked several times. "Anyone critical?"

"No."

Her shoulders sagged, and Mary wilted against the couch. "Thank You, Lord."

Matthews scanned his notes. "It has been confirmed the sprinkler system was tampered with. From what we can piece together, four red smoke bombs went off pretty close together. I suspect someone used a detonator to set them off. The back part of the theater has been searched, since the fire didn't reach that far and the devices were attached to the seats. Several hours earlier the theater owner had had a dog sniff for bombs before setting up for the event. Only people who had been vetted were allowed inside after the stage was set up. The doors were locked and guards posted until the event opened. People were checked as they came in."

"So how were the smoke bombs planted?" T.J. asked, not liking where this was going.

"There are security cameras, but not all over the theater. Interestingly, the smoke bombs were placed where the cameras didn't reach."

"Inside job?" Had this job been hired out to a pro? T.J. began to wonder if there was more going on here.

"I think so, and we're looking at staff employees, but that will take time. I'll keep you informed if we get any kind of lead. Mary, Paul, can you think of anyone who is holding a grudge against you?"

"You don't think it's our message?" Paul asked.

"It's possible, but I think this is tied up in a more personal angle." Chloe rose and prowled the room, stopping to stare out the window.

"I have to agree with Chloe." T.J. leaned forward and placed his elbows on his thighs, clasping his hands together.

"No, when we aren't writing or speaking, we have a quiet life at our ranch. We treat our employees like friends."

T.J. stood across from the detective. "We're leaving early tomorrow morning for the Zimmermans' ranch between Houston and San Antonio. We're making a slight detour to pick up their sixteen-year-old son at Bethany Academy in Houston. You have my number. Call if you find out anything."

"Will do." Matthews nodded toward the couple then Chloe. "I've got more I have to do tonight so I need to get back, but let me know if you can think of anyone who would want to hurt you."

T.J. saw the detective out of the house and waited until he went through the gate before returning to the living room. "I'll take first watch again tonight since I'll be driving to-morrow. Mary, are you going to call your son and let him know what you're doing?"

"Yes, now that we know we can leave. I was afraid Detective Matthews would need us to stay, but I really have no idea why this is happening, especially today. What was done was bolder than in Paris or at the church the other day." She delved into her pocket. "Can I use my phone? He'll know that number. In fact, he's probably expecting a call after what happened and wondering why I'm not answering my cell. At least I was able to call the school and let them know we were okay since he was on a field trip."

T.J. handed her his untraceable one. "Use this one. If he wonders why you're calling on a different phone, chalk it up to me being cautious."

Paul came to sit beside Mary while she made the call to their son. T.J. left the room with Chloe to give the couple some privacy. In the entry hall, he turned toward her. "Ready to go?"

"As I said at the other house, I haven't unpacked. Maybe at the ranch I actually will."

"On the ride to the ranch, we need to have a conversation about how the ranch operates. Who does what? Who works there? How long? I know Mary called her cousin, who takes care of the home, and Paul talked with his foreman to let him know he would be returning earlier than expected to the ranch."

"Mary has mentioned a Vickie Campbell. Is she the cousin?"

"Yes. The foreman is Zach Bradley. I overheard Paul arguing with him about selling some cattle. He told him to hold off until he got home."

Chloe's forehead scrunched. "Paul's the owner."

"Who is gone a lot of the time. Maybe Zach

is used to running the ranch without someone looking over his shoulder."

"I'm just glad that Mary and Paul called off the tour, but they are doing a TV interview after they get back home. The TV crew has agreed to film it at the ranch, so at least the Zimmermans won't have to go to the studio." Chloe kneaded her hand into her neck. That had been to appease Nancy, who was throwing a fit about canceling the interview tomorrow morning. "But if it's not safe at the ranch, that TV interview will be canceled, too, no matter what Nancy says."

"You're still tense."

"Your powers of observation are amazing." A twinkle sparkled in her eyes. "I'm trying to loosen those knots the best way I can."

"I can help." He winked.

"If I can't work them out, I might take you up on that."

"Good. Whatever makes my partner—"

Mary appeared at the living room entrance, tears gleaming in her eyes. "Aaron insists no one is after him, just us. He refuses to leave school and come to the ranch. He hung up on me."

SEVEN

Passing through the iron gates of the Sizzling Z Ranch, Chloe noted their sturdy structure, a plus as far as security was concerned, but the black fence along the property where the highway ran could easily be vaulted. From a distance she spied a large two-story redbrick antebellum home. The white trim stood out between the trees—mostly pine. Not far from the house, maybe two hundred yards, sat a black barn.

As they neared the home, a thin woman, who was five foot seven or eight inches and about forty years old, came out onto the verandah. Her blond hair pulled back in a tight bun, she held her hand up to shield the sun slanting across the porch.

T.J. parked his car in front. "Is that your cousin Vickie?"

"Yes. I don't know what we would do without her. She keeps the house running smoothly, especially when we're gone," Mary said, sandwiched between Chloe and her pouting son in the backseat.

The second the vehicle stopped, Aaron Zimmerman shoved open the door and scrambled from the Jeep.

Mary climbed out of the car. "Aaron."

He threw a glare over his shoulder and kept going while Chloe quickly exited the vehicle and came around to Mary.

She leaned close to Chloe. "Sorry about the attitude. He has always felt like he's living in the limelight because of who we are, and now he feels even more restricted." She trailed after her son with Chloe right behind her.

The sixteen-year-old pushed past Vickie and charged through the entrance to his home. The sound of him stomping up the steps echoed through the large foyer, which was the size of Chloe's living and dining room at her apartment. Mary went after her son, waving Chloe back.

She respected Mary's desire to talk to Aaron alone, so she would give mother and son a minute, then follow. She hadn't had a chance to even canvass the house and see what kind of security was in place. The description the Zimmermans had given them on the way hadn't told her much. They had a several-year-old alarm system. That could mean anything. The front gate was controlled by a remote or a keyed-in number and remained locked. That was good, but then as she'd observed that wouldn't stop a person on foot.

A minute later, Chloe started up the steps, glancing back while Paul and T.J. brought in the luggage. Vickie closed the front door behind them, then peered at Chloe. Vickie welcomed Chloe with a warm smile before turning her attention to Paul and T.J.

On the second floor, there was a long hallway to the right and left with four rooms on either side. She strolled down the corridor to the right but couldn't hear any voices. She traversed the left hall to the end and checked out the barn about two hundred yards away as well as the lock on the window. This house's configuration was similar to the first house they'd stayed in Dallas, which didn't leave her with a comfortable feeling.

The sound of a shrill, angry voice pierced the air, coming from the nearest room to her right. The door slammed open and Aaron rushed into the hallway, sending her a narrow-eyed look before stalking off toward the staircase.

Chloe moved toward the room to see if Mary was inside and all right. She came face to face with Mary, an ashen tinge to her features. Her client tried to shrug and smile. Both attempts collapsed.

"I'm a psychologist and should be prepared for my son's rebellious behavior. I certainly counseled enough parents concerning that." Tears returned to Mary's eyes, and she averted her head, swiping her hand across her cheeks.

"I didn't eavesdrop—my job is just to be with you and keep you safe."

"I've got to have some freedom in my own home. Paul said he would do what needed to be done so that the family could move about without always having someone with us, especially for Aaron's sake. I'm not sure what he would do otherwise. He was furious with us this morning for staying on tour as long as we did. I assured him we were all right, but that didn't appease him."

"You and Paul are celebrities in a sense, and I've seen this before. That can be hard on the children. I imagine T.J. has stories about the children of the vice president rebelling over their confinement. We'll tour the house and grounds and make this work for you and your son."

Mary enveloped her in a hug. "Bless you. This has been difficult on all of us. I have a hard time thinking about someone out there hating me so much he would set fire to the theater and risk harming so many innocent people."

"The fire still could be an accident. I'm calling Detective Matthews later to see what the arson investigator said."

"I guess we need to have hope. That's what helps people keep going forward. Please tell Paul I've decided to lie down."

"Where's your room?"

Mary pointed to the door across from her son's. "I thought I would have you stay in the room next to ours and T.J. in the one beside my son's. Is that okay?"

"Perfect. Where does Vickie stay?"

"She has the room at the far end of the hall."

"How long has she been living here?"

"Ever since she had to file for bankruptcy three years ago when her business failed. She had no place to go, and we were happy to open our home to her. Since she didn't want a free ride, she asked to be the housekeeper when our other one left unexpectedly. She's a jewel. She also keeps the ranch books and works with Zach to make sure it runs smoothly. Now do you see why we are so appreciative for both of their help?" Mary took a few steps and opened her door. "I'll be down later."

"Let me come inside and at least check out your room."

Mary chuckled. "I don't think anyone can get under my bed."

Chloe looked around, checking to make sure the windows were locked, before crossing to the bathroom, drawing the shower curtain back then inspecting the huge walk-in closet. She'd seen bedrooms that were smaller.

"Anyone behind the dresses?" Mary's mouth tipped up for a second, then quavered. "What have we done so wrong that we deserve this kind of harassment?"

Chloe closed the space between them and took her client's hands. "Some people don't need a good reason. In their mind they have twisted everything around to suit their need."

"Thank you, Chloe. I'm usually the one holding someone else up."

Chloe gave her hands a squeeze, then

walked into the hallway. "Rest. You'll stay safe if I have anything to do with it."

When she descended the staircase, T.J. and Paul stood in the middle of the foyer next to the round glass table with a huge floral arrangement. The scent of roses, lilies and some kind of flower she didn't know the name of drifted to her as she paused in front of the two men deep in conversation.

T.J. smiled at her. "Is Mary okay?"

"Yes." Chloe glanced around the foyer and the surrounding rooms. "Where did Aaron go?"

Paul's thick eyebrows slashed almost together. "Knowing my son, he's left the house out the back. He'll probably go to the stable, which is not far from the barn."

T.J. straightened. "Is he going riding?"

"If he's going there, it's to ride."

"He can't. At least not without one of us with him. We don't know what we're dealing with. The person might have been trying just to stop your tour. If so, then nothing else will happen, but most likely there's more to it." T.J. looked at Chloe. "Do you want to go after him or should I?"

"I will."

"If you think my family is in danger, not just me and Mary, do we need to bring in bodyguards for him and Vickie?" Paul asked, his frown deepening. "Because I don't think Aaron will stay inside the whole time. When he comes to the ranch, he spends a lot of his time outside. He even helps Zach and the other hands with the cattle."

Chloe gritted her teeth. "He needs to be made to realize the seriousness of the situation."

Paul exhaled audibly. "At the school when we talked with him in his room while he was packing, he was so angry. He seems to be that way all the time lately. I've tried everything with him, but nothing seems to work. If I ground him to the house, he'll find a way to escape his prison, because that's what he'll think it is."

"Since you've agreed to get a couple of security dogs, I can bring in some men to handle them and walk the perimeter outside. We need to be prepared for the long haul."

"While you two discuss the issue, I'd better get Aaron before he rides off." Chloe headed for the front door.

"Do you ride?" Paul called out.

She swiveled around at the exit. "Yes, so I'll go after him if I have to. This will be a good time to meet some of your men."

Beyond the barn, Chloe spied the stable, a long black building. Aaron led a horse out of the open double doors. He patted the animal, then hiked his foot into the stirrup. Five yards away. Instead of calling out, she hurried her pace.

As he mounted, Chloe reached his side and snatched hold of the reins and then the bridle. "You aren't going anywhere. In case you didn't understand your parents earlier, there is a madman out there bent on hurting them."

"But not me."

"How do you know that? One of the worst ways to hurt a parent is to do something to their child."

"Just great! The one thing I enjoy at the ranch, riding, and now I can't even do it because of them."

He sent her a look that screamed he intended to defy his parents anyway.

She shot him a hard stare. "Don't even think it."

"Think what? Are you a mind reader now?" the boy sneered.

"One of my many talents. You're thinking by the time I could get a horse saddled you'd be long gone." She narrowed her eyes. "I'm prepared to hold on if you try. Are you ready to face the consequences?"

"What?" His glare challenged her.

Inching more toward the middle of the horse while holding on, Chloe watched for the slightest indication he would try to ride away. A tic in his jaw line twitched as he sat forward and kicked the sides of his horse. Letting go of the reins, she vaulted into the saddle right behind him and locked her arms around him. The mare set out in a canter.

"Where are we going?"

Aaron pulled back on the reins, his shoulder hunching over. "Nowhere."

"Good choice."

"I don't have a choice. I can hardly breathe. Can you loosen your hold?"

"Are you going to get off?"

He huffed. "Yes. It's not like I could get very far with you hounding me."

After Chloe slid off, keeping her grip on the saddle, Aaron dismounted, anger raging in his eyes.

"Take care of your horse, then we'll go back to the house."

As he removed the saddle, he said, "You must ride a lot to be able to do what you did."

"I grew up around horses, so yes, you might say I have."

He looked her up and down. "You're quick."

"I'm a bodyguard. I need to be."

He finished tending his mare in silence, and then turned it loose in the paddock next to the stable before storming toward the house. On the trek back, Chloe assessed the outside security issues. Most would be taken care of with dogs and a guard patrolling. But nearer the antebellum home, she noticed the lack of lights for the grounds. A brightly lit place was less likely to be hit.

Aaron disappeared inside, the back door slamming closed. Now all she and T.J. needed was for everyone to follow the security procedures. That might be the hardest part of this assignment.

That night, Chloe took her seat next to Mary at the dining room table while T.J. sat between Aaron and Paul. Vickie rushed through the swinging doors and put the last dish in the middle of the table for eight, then eased onto her chair on the other side of Chloe.

Mary reached for her son's and Chloe's hands, bowing her head. "I'd like to say the blessing tonight." After everyone joined hands, she continued. "Dear Heavenly Father, thank You for delivering my son, husband and me safely home. Please heal Joy, Samuel, Bill and Kitty so they can be home with their families, too. Thank You for sending Chloe and T.J. to protect us. Paul and I forgive the person who is after us. Heal his hurt and anger. And last, bless this food that Vickie prepared for us. Amen."

Quickly releasing his mother's hand, Aaron kept his head down as though he'd found an interesting spot on his plate. Since coming back from the stable four hours ago, he'd been in his room, refusing to come out when his mother had tried to coax him to join them.

"Who are Joy, Samuel, Bill and Kitty?" Vickie asked as she passed the platter of roast beef.

"We found out those are the people still in the hospital from yesterday's fire." Paul took the meat from Vickie, speared a thick, juicy slice, then gave the platter to T.J.

Aaron lifted his chin and looked at his dad. "There were people hurt?"

"Yes, I'm surprised you didn't hear about it. It's been splashed all over the news. Some were injured and taken to the hospital."

"I don't look at the news. All it talks about

is what's bad in this world. I didn't know anything had happened to you until the school told me and then said you two were all right." Aaron spooned the broccoli rice casserole onto his plate and then gave the vegetable dish to his mother without even looking her way.

Chloe watched the terse exchange between Aaron and Paul, most of the tension—not just tension, but anger—coming from the son. Even though he was upset at his mom and dad, it was strange Aaron didn't turn on a TV to see what was going on or go on the internet. But then, when did she? She didn't purposefully check the news every day, especially when she was on a job, unless it directly affected the assignment.

"Have you heard from Detective Matthews about how the fire got started?" Mary asked Chloe while cutting her roast.

"Not yet. With all that happened at the theater, he's been busy tracking down leads."

"Any good ones?" Vickie sipped some water.

"A couple, from what he told me this afternoon. I promised I wouldn't bother him until later this evening. He was interviewing the people behind the stage. The woman he carried out shouldn't have been there. She's disappeared. We think she was filling in for a sick employee of the event-planning company." Chloe had just gotten off the phone with Rob right before dinner and hadn't gotten a chance to tell T.J. or the Zimmermans. He was going to talk to the arson investigator and would elaborate when he called her after that meeting.

Mary sat forward. "Then they might actually find the person?"

"Maybe. It could be nothing, or it could lead to the person behind this. The Dallas police will continue to investigate every piece of evidence." Chloe scooped up some broccoli and rice. "Vickie, this meal is delicious."

Vickie grinned and started to say something, but Aaron cut in, "Do we have to sit here and talk about this all the time? It's bad enough I'm a prisoner here in my own home."

"Actually, son, that's a good suggestion. When we're eating, we won't from now on." Paul swept his gaze around the table.

Silence fell over the table as everyone dug into their food. Except Aaron. He toyed with his meat and vegetables, moving them around on his plate, not even pleased at what his father had said.

The doorbell rang.

Chloe's hand tightened on her fork as she finished her last bite. Sitting nearest the foyer, she rose and glanced at Paul. "Are you expecting anyone?"

"That'll be Zach. I told him to come up to the house when he was through for the day. We have some business to discuss. He just returned from being gone for a week and some issues need to be tied up."

Chloe started for the entry hall. "What does he look like?"

"Tall, thin with salt-and-pepper hair." Paul stood. "I'll let him in."

Chloe whirled around. "No. Either T.J. or I will do that, even with a person you know."

Paul covered the distance between them. "Surely you don't think it's Zach. He's worked here for years."

"Where was he last week?"

Paul's mouth dropped open. "I've known him for eight years."

In the foyer, Chloe stopped. "Was he on vacation?"

"No, his father was ill and not doing well. He asked for the time off to go see him in Dallas."

"He was there at the same time you were?"

Paul frowned, folding his arms over his chest. "It's not Zach."

"Still, I need the information to make sure he was where he said he would be." Chloe put her hand on the knob, then pulled it open to keep Paul from responding. It was always hard for a person to realize someone close might be the one after them. She and T.J. had to look at all possibilities, especially the ones in direct contact with Mary and Paul.

As she let the ranch foreman into the house, T.J. came to the dining room entrance. After

Paul introduced her and she shook Zach's hand, T.J. crossed to the foreman and greeted him.

"I missed you at the barn a couple of hours ago." T.J. studied Zach.

The foreman removed his cowboy hat and held it by the brim. "I went into town to see about some feed problems."

"Come in, Zach. Let's go to my office. I'll have Vickie bring in coffee and a piece of the chocolate cake she baked today."

T.J. strolled behind the two men, but Paul paused at the end of the hallway that led to the back part of the place. "You don't need to come. I don't want Zach to think I suspect him, because I don't. Stay here. Please."

T.J. nodded, but when he turned toward Chloe, his jaw was set in a hard line. He walked to her. "They don't really understand the danger they're in. They think now that they're home everything will return to normal."

"I know. That's the most dangerous time—

when they let down their guard. I'll try to get that point across to Mary again."

"And I'll talk with Paul. But he's a lot like his son. I caught him earlier going out the back to go see Zach. He'd forgotten to tell me he was going to the barn. Freedom is hard to give up."

"We do every day. We're as much a prisoner as they are."

T.J. chuckled. "But we're in control, dictating the rules."

"I'm not hungry anymore." Aaron's loud voice wafted to Chloe. "At least I can go upstairs by myself." He appeared in the doorway to the dining room. "I would appreciate no one bothering me." As he swung around, his glare drilled into T.J., then Chloe. "That includes you two." Then he tramped up the stairs.

"Good thing there's only one child or my patience would have been exhausted by now."

T.J. leaned close to her ear. "Mine was gone about an hour after I met Aaron. And there was a time I wanted to be a father.

Being around that boy has definitely made me reconsider."

The idea T.J. had considered having children flushed her cheeks, heat spreading down her face. She wanted a family, too—still did. "I agree. Having children is a serious decision. Once my mother told me I should take care of young children before I decide, so I babysat a lot when I was Aaron's age. Young children are a piece of cake next to a teen like Aaron. I think taking care of teenagers should be the criteria."

"I wonder where all his anger comes from—how long he's been this way."

"I had a cousin who hated the world his freshman, sophomore and junior years in high school. She actually became bearable during her senior year. I'll see what else Mary has to say about her son. It might help us protect him better if we know where he's coming from." She turned to head into the dining room.

T.J. fell into step beside her, his hand

casually at the small of her back. "I'll see what Paul has to say, too."

The brief connection between her and T.J. spurred her pulse to a faster rate. How had they gotten on the subject of having children? Dangerous territory when she was trying to keep her emotional distance. But it was hard when they fell into such an easy partnership—a true team.

T.J. moved through the living room, checking each window to make sure it was locked, a habit he'd formed because once one of them had been unlocked. In that situation, it had turned out a maid was working for the person targeting the man he was protecting as a Secret Service agent. It never hurt to be extracautious.

For a moment he lingered in front of the window overlooking the verandah and yard. He would be relieved with the addition of the dogs and outside guards. The number of people he and Chloe were guarding had doubled, not to mention one was rebellious and hostile about his situation. He'd protected enough family members as a Secret Service agent to know a young person didn't always see the danger until it was too late.

He'd chosen the right partner with Chloe. They had fallen into a pattern that complemented each other.

But as he'd waited to hear that she was out of the building and safe, the fear he'd felt had made it clear that his feelings for her weren't dead. At the moment, his life was at a crossroads. He'd always known what he wanted and had been focused on that goal. Now he wasn't sure. Should he walk away from what he'd been doing all his life—guarding people in danger—or continue in some other capacity? In the middle of all this, he certainly didn't need to fall in love with Chloe again. He trusted her as a partner, but to trust her with his heart was totally different. Or was it? He didn't like this confusion, this lack of control.

"I'm going to bed," Chloe said as she entered the living room.

The soft sound of her voice penetrated his thoughts and only heightened his dilemma. They had been good together once, but it hadn't worked out. Did he want to be hurt again? He could still remember the pain he'd felt when she hadn't come to Washington.

He rotated toward her slowly. "It'll be nice when we have a guard outside, patrolling the grounds. It'll give us a chance to get a good night's sleep. At least I hope. I can go without sleep for a while, but it does catch up with me eventually."

Chloe came further into the room. "All this emotion can be draining. Earlier when I talked to Mary about Aaron, I could see she was barely holding it together."

"It's been a rough week and her son isn't helping things." T.J. walked to the last window and examined the lock. "Did she tell you anything about Aaron that might help us?"

She joined him, inches away. "I don't know about helping us, but she did share something concerning Aaron. He had a younger brother who died about seven years ago. Aaron took it as hard as Mary and Paul did. As a result of Mary and Paul's grief, they turned all their energy to helping others."

Her vanilla scent, the same one she'd had when they had dated, surrounded him with memories. The first time they had met. The first time he'd kissed her. The last day, when they had parted. A constriction in his chest reminded him of the hurt that had stayed with him for years.

"How long has he been at the Bethany Academy?"

"Since he was a freshman. The school he went to wasn't academically challenging, so they sent him to Bethany Academy. It's close enough that he can come for the weekends when he wants."

"Does he like the school?" He started for the foyer, needing some space before he decided to see if she still kissed as well as she had nine years ago.

"She thinks so, but she confessed her son doesn't confide in her like he used to when he was a young boy. But that's often normal with any teenager." She trailed behind him, that soft, husky voice tempting him to take her into his arms.

T.J. held them tight against his side. The brighter lights in the entry hall sobered him. They were working, not on a date. He turned toward her. "Have you guarded many teenagers?" He needed to keep focused on business.

"I don't know if you consider it a lot, but in four years, maybe ten or so, mostly girls, and a couple of boys. One was thirteen. The other sixteen. The thirteen-year-old was a challenge." She grinned, two dimples appearing in her cheeks. "But Aaron could prove to top him." Her eyes widened. "You aren't leaving me to deal with him all the time. Surely we can take turns."

"I have a feeling he'll respond to you better than me. A beautiful woman usually does that to a sixteen-year-old," T.J. said with a chuckle.

Occasionally he'd seen Chloe blush, and this was one of those times. As though it had a will of its own his hand lifted, and he brushed a finger across her cheek. "You *are* beautiful. Inside and out. Because of you, I became serious about my relationship with the Lord. Maybe this is the reason we met again. That faith has wavered."

"Why?"

"Life and the things I've seen. People aren't who they say they are. I knew that before I became a Secret Service agent, but some of my assignments made that very clear."

"Do you want to talk about it?"

Though he wanted to inch closer, T.J. stepped back. "I can't, and sometimes that's the problem. What I saw as an agent remains a secret. That's part of the job."

"I've often used Kyra as a sounding board when I needed one having to do with my job. Sometimes we just need to talk it out. If you can't with another person and I can certainly understand that with the job you had, then talk to the Lord about it. He's always there to listen."

"Praying."

"Not exactly. Sharing your thoughts with him isn't always praying."

"I've missed you," slipped out of his mouth before he could stop it. Then, as though he needed to qualify it, he added, "I've always been able to tell you things I never could others."

One corner of her mouth tilted upward. "We did have that once."

"Yes, maybe—"

"Chloe. T.J." Mary's frantic voice came from the second-floor landing. "I went to say good night to Aaron. He's not in his room, and his window is wide-open."

EIGHT

Chloe whirled around and raced up the stairs.

Fear held Mary rigid, her hand clutching the railing. "He's been here. He took my son."

"None of your bedrooms can be accessed without a tall ladder, and Zach took care of that for us. They're locked up in the barn."

T.J. came up behind Chloe. "Where's Paul?"

"I'm here. What's going on?" Paul left his room and stood across from Aaron's, confusion clouding his expression.

"Aaron isn't in his room," Mary said in a clogged voice. "Remember how that person came into the house in Dallas. He's done it again. He's..."

"Aaron's downstairs." Paul bridged the

short distance to Mary and took her in his embrace. "I doubt someone brought his own ladder, and ours are at the barn locked in the shed."

Chloe hurried toward the boy's room. "He isn't downstairs."

The color washed from Paul's face. "Then he's hiding to make us worry."

Chloe and T.J. entered to find the window wide-open, the curtains blowing in the cold wind. Careful not to touch anything, Chloe made a full circle while T.J. pushed back the sheers and examined the window and outside it. She noticed the bed was minus its sheets.

"There's a rope made out of sheets that goes most of the way to the ground. I suspect Aaron snuck out." T.J. faced the couple as they stood in the entrance. "Would he go to a friend's house? Anywhere you can think of?"

Paul shook his head. "Most of his friends are at school. He's lost contact with the ones he had around here."

"Except for Brett. He might be with him.

We can call him and see," Mary said, her chest rising and falling rapidly.

Chloe was concerned for her client. "Mary, you need to sit down. We'll take care of this. He's most likely being a teenager and doing what he wants."

"But you don't know for sure."

"Paul, call the sheriff and let him know Aaron is gone," T.J. said. "Let him know what's going on. I have a feeling he's aware of what happened in Dallas. I'm going outside to inspect the ground below the window. Chloe, go through the house in case Aaron slipped by us." T.J. headed for the stairs.

Paul settled his arm over Mary's trembling shoulder and pressed her close. "I'll see to Mary and call the sheriff. We're friends. I'm sure he'll want to come."

Chloe glanced around. "Where's Vickie?"

"Probably in her room. Sometimes Aaron will talk to her, especially when he's mad at us. We'll get dressed and come downstairs." Paul escorted his wife into their bedroom.

"I'll check there first." Chloe strode to

the other end of the long hall and knocked on the woman's door. When it opened and Vickie peered out, Chloe asked, "Is Aaron with you?"

"No." She stepped out into the corridor, dressed for bed with a robe on. "What's happened?"

"We believe he went out his window. Hopefully on his own."

"How?"

As Chloe explained, the deep lines in Vickie's forehead faded.

"Aaron has done that before."

"Mary and Paul didn't say anything about that."

"That's because they don't know. It happened last summer. He was grounded, but they were away for a weekend retreat. I discovered him sneaking back into the house and he told me everything. He thought his parents were too strict and he had plans to meet Brett, so he did anyway."

"Please go tell Paul and Mary while I check the rest of the house."

As Chloe descended the stairs, she thought of finding T.J. outside and letting him know, then decided instead to wait until he came back in. No point in having two people wandering around in the dark.

T.J. shone his flashlight over the ground directly under Aaron's bedroom window. Signs of the same tennis-shoe size indicated only one person was involved. Aaron. It didn't surprise him when he thought of the teen's behavior today.

He looked up and made a full circle trying to see beyond the few security lights into the night beyond. A noise like an engine starting to the left caught T.J.'s attention. He jogged toward it, sweeping his flashlight in front of him the farther away from the house he went.

Is that a pickup parked off the drive? The hairs on the back of his neck prickled. He spun around as something hard connected with his head. His legs gave out, and the black swallowed him.

* * *

Chloe paced the foyer at the bottom of the staircase and for the sixth time glanced at her watch. More than ever, she wanted to go out and see where T.J. was, but if he was in trouble, she needed to be here to protect the Zimmermans and Vickie. She checked the gun she'd strapped to her side. He'd been gone ten minutes. He shouldn't have been gone that long.

She mounted the steps and made her way toward Mary and Paul's bedroom. The door was open and Vickie stood just inside.

"I need Zach and a few of the men to search for T.J. He hasn't come back and all he was going to do was look around under Aaron's window."

Paul picked up the phone. "I'll call him."

"I'm returning to the hall and positioning myself on the stairs. Keep this door open unless you hear me tell you to shut it."

Mary's face whitened. "It's happening again."

As she moved into the hallway, Chloe

looked back. "I don't know what's going on, but we need to be prepared for anything."

In the distance, T.J. heard the sound of a vehicle driving away. His eyes fluttered open. The scent of earth filled his nostrils. The feel of grass cushioned his left cheek. Bright lights—a beacon that called to him—shone through the darkness that encased him. But the one sensation he couldn't ignore was the pain hammering against his skull.

For a moment he tried to remember what had happened. Where he was? Why he was here with a gong thundering in his head?

Aaron. Gone. Slowly the words filtered through the pain, and he struggled to sit up. He remembered the vehicle—a pickup, he thought—and the noise of it leaving. He couldn't have passed out for more than a few seconds.

The black spun around.

Closing his eyes, he sat still, trying to right his twirling world.

"T.J.," someone shouted through the fog surrounding his brain.

"Over here," he said while he eased his eyelids up halfway, the sound of his voice thundering through his head.

Circles of light illustrated his whereabouts. He averted his head, panning the area as he pieced together what had occurred.

A vehicle had started. He'd gone to investigate. Then someone must have hit him from behind. He felt the back of his head and winced when he encountered a sticky wetness.

As flashlights came toward T.J., he lowered his chin while his eyes adjusted to the brightness.

When the ranch foreman knelt in front of him, he asked, "What happened?"

T.J. looked at Zach and a ranch hand named Shane behind the foreman. "Someone knocked me out." As he said those words, alarm rippled through him. Chloe and the others could be in danger. "I need to get to the house." He tried to rise—too quickly—and collapsed back to the ground.

"I'd suggest slow and easy." Zach moved around to examine the back of his head. "You're gonna have a doozy of a headache."

He didn't have time for an injury. He pushed himself to his feet with Zach next to him, poised to help if needed. "Have you seen Aaron?"

"Not since he came to the stable earlier."

T.J. started for the Zimmermans' home, his gait slow but steady. The nearer they came, the faster the haze over his brain faded. Zach made a call to Paul and let him know T.J. was all right and coming back to the house.

The door flew open, and Chloe positioned herself in the entrance, one hand on her gun. She took one look at him, and her severe expression melted into relief, but a slight frown still tugged at her mouth.

"What kind of trouble did you manage to get into? It was a simple task. Check the footprints under the window." She settled her fist on her waist.

"Someone else had a different plan." T.J. cocked a grin. "But I'm fine, as you can see."

Chloe motioned with her hand. "Turn around and let me see for myself." She sucked in a deep breath. "Your idea of fine is different from mine. So tell me what happened." She stepped to the side to allow him inside. "Thanks, Zach. Can you and your men check the grounds out from the house and let me know if you find anything unusual? The sheriff is on his way."

Once she'd closed and locked the front door, T.J. made his way to the stairs and sat. "I heard a vehicle start and went to investigate. Then, a minute later, I saw a pickup stopped on the side of the drive."

"Did you see Aaron?"

"No. I didn't see anyone. The person who hit me came up from behind."

Chloe took out her cell phone and made a call. "Zach, this is Chloe. Check to see if any vehicles are gone. Maybe a pickup." She paused, her eyebrows scrunching. "Just a minute. I'll ask him."

"Can you describe the pickup?" She held her cell between them so Zach could hear.

"No, I didn't get close enough. I heard it coming from the left side of the house. I went around the corner and started into the yard. The lighting over there isn't good. I saw a tire and was lifting my flashlight to get a better look at the vehicle when I was struck."

"Did you get that? Okay. Thanks." Chloe slipped her phone back in her pocket. "Zach said that's where the old Ford F-150 is kept. Aaron drives it when he's home."

"So Aaron hit me?"

"Maybe. What did you find with the footprints?"

"Only one set under the window, which leads me to think it was Aaron. Probably alone, but maybe with a friend."

"I'll go up and get Mary and Paul. We'll need a description and license number if the Ford F-150 is gone. Then you're going to the hospital."

"No. I'm okay. I promise I'll tell you if the signs of a concussion worsen. I'm not dizzy anymore, and I can take something for my headache. See if they have something for one. Aaron may have decided to leave, but he's still in danger. He's a kid. He doesn't realize the danger he's in. The kidnapping of a child is a parent's worst nightmare."

"Don't say anything to Mary or Paul. They are already beside themselves." Chloe ascended the stairs and disappeared down the hall.

T.J. clutched the railing and pulled himself to his feet. There was a guest bathroom off the foyer. He went in and did the best he could to wash the blood off the side of his head behind his left ear. Grimacing, he patted the area with a wet cloth.

When he reappeared in the foyer, Paul, Mary and Vickie stood at the bottom of the steps.

Vickie saw his injury and scurried toward the kitchen, muttering about a bandage and some pain relief in the first-aid kit.

"The sheriff is almost here. Aaron has a 2006 Ford F-150. This is the license number." Paul handed T.J. a slip of paper. "The pickup can't go over fifty miles an hour without problems. It's really only good for around here or in town."

"Where do you think he went?" T.J. dug into his pocket for his set of keys.

"Not Brett's. I talked with the kid's parents. I would guess back to school, but then I really don't know my son as well as I should. I didn't think he would be stupid enough to leave." Frustration and concern weaved through Paul's words.

Chloe snatched the keys from T.J. "He hasn't been gone that long. I'm leaving and heading back toward Houston. I can make up some time in your car and possibly catch up with him." She held out her hand. "The license number, please."

"I'm going with you."

"You can't. Someone has to stay back here with our clients, and if you have a problem, you need to be near medical help." Chloe took the paper from T.J. and then turned to Paul.

"If you need to, ask the sheriff for assistance keeping you all safe."

"He'll give it to me. Bring my son home, then we'll have a heart-to-heart about his leaving." Paul set his mouth in a deep frown, but his eyes were full of concern—two intense emotions fighting for dominance.

Chloe walked toward the front door.

"Wait," T.J. called out and made his way to her.

"Call me every twenty minutes and let me know what's going on."

She grinned. "I'm not going to take offense to that, but I'm a big girl and have been a bodyguard for years."

"That won't stop me from worrying."

Her smile grew. "I know. I'd worry about you, too." Then she was out the door.

"There you are," Vickie said behind him. "C'mon and sit down so I can tend to your injury. I've patched up the ranch hands and have become quite good at doing it."

T.J. released his frustration in a long, drawn-out exhalation.

* * *

With her cell phone hooked up to T.J.'s car, Chloe could call safely and still go sixty-five. The sheriff had arrived as she left the ranch and was having his two deputies work with the cowhands to search the area.

Checking in with T.J. for the first time, Chloe scanned the cars as she approached and passed them. "What if Aaron is somewhere at the ranch having a good laugh right about now?"

"He won't be laughing when I get through with him."

"You okay?"

"I've had better days. Paul has a friend who's a doctor. He's paying us a call and will take a look. If I didn't agree, Paul was going to have the sheriff drive me to the hospital."

"A doctor making a house call? I guess it pays to know people. Did the sheriff put a BOLO out on Aaron and the Ford F-150?"

"Yes, and he and his deputies are canvassing the area, especially around the main house."

"Good. Take it easy. Bye."

As she started to hang up, she heard T.J. say, "Don't forget to call in twenty minutes."

Chloe punched the off button and increased her speed by five miles per hour. She didn't like being away from her client, but then she guessed Aaron was their client, too—whether he liked it or not.

Ten minutes later, she saw the black Ford F-150 with the correct license plate number. She came right up behind him and flashed her lights. The truck picked up speed. She easily kept up with it, and after five miles, she passed Aaron to force him to stop. Slamming on her brakes, she turned the wheel and blocked the two-lane highway. Aaron came to a halt a couple of feet from T.J.'s Jeep.

She got out of the car, and when the teen opened his door, she shouted, "Park on the side of the road. You're coming back with me."

"I can drive back." Frustration and something she couldn't quite put her finger on filled his voice. Fear? If he had been afraid, then why did he run away?

"No. Move it now." She poured all her anger into her words, determined the kid understood she wouldn't put up with his antics. Part of her prepared to chase after him in the opposite direction, if need be.

But to her surprise, the teenager did as he was told and stormed to T.J.'s Jeep, glaring over the roof at her. "I can make my own decisions. I'll be seventeen in a few months. I *need* to go back to Houston."

"Then start acting like the mature adult that you claim you are and get in my car. Your life is more important than attending school at the moment. Your parents have it worked out with Bethany Academy. Your friends will understand. If not, they aren't your friends."

He wrenched open the door and climbed in. Chloe peered up at the nearly full moon. *Lord, I need Your help to get through to this child the danger he could be in.*

As she restarted the car, she slanted a look at Aaron. "What did you think your parents would do when they discovered you were gone? Let you stay at school in danger? They love you."

"They have a great way of showing it," Aaron mumbled and averted his head to stare out the side window.

"Before you go into your pouting routine, use the phone and call your parents to let them know you're coming back to the ranch with me."

"You do it. I don't feel like talking to them. I want to be in Houston."

One. Two. Three. Giving up counting to ten, Chloe chewed on her bottom lip to keep her retort inside. At the moment, Aaron wasn't listening to anything she said.

Chloe called the ranch. "Mary, I've got your son with me. We're heading back to the ranch. We left the truck at the side of the road. Someone should go and pick it up tomorrow."

"Thank You, Lord. I'm so glad you found him. Tell him I love him and don't want anything to happen to him."

"I will. How's T.J. doing?" She wished she were there in person to make sure he was okay.

"The doc says he should be all right, but if anything changes, he'll need to go to the hospital for tests."

"See you all in about half an hour." When she hung up, she looked toward Aaron.

With his shoulders hunched, he'd almost turned his whole body away.

"Did you hit T.J. over the head so you could get away?"

"No," he mumbled, hunkering over even more, his arms folded over his chest.

Chloe suspected if he could crawl under the seat, he would have. "You're the only one who had a reason to."

He swiveled toward her. "I'm not lying! I didn't!" His shouts bombarded her. The fury flowed off him.

She gritted her teeth and concentrated on getting them back to the ranch. Aaron wasn't out of danger. There was thirty miles between here and the ranch.

* * *

After a search of the area around the house, T.J. and Paul went to talk to Sheriff Landon and Zach in the living room. When they entered, T.J. found the sheriff, a deputy and Shane Clapton, who had been with Zach earlier.

"Where's Zach?" T.J. asked, not sure of Shane's position at the ranch other than ranch hand.

"I fill in for the foreman when Zach's busy somewhere else. One of the horses is giving birth and there's a problem." The man, who was about thirty-five years old with a receding hairline, glanced at Paul. "Zach can handle it, Mr. Zimmerman. He told me to tell you not to worry."

"I'm sure he can. Did you find anything to explain who attacked T.J.?"

Shane glanced at the sheriff, who answered, "No signs. There are a lot of footprints around in the dirt near where you were found, but a lot of them were Zach's and Shane's. The tennis-shoe print under the window matched the one where the car was, which I'm gonna assume is your son's."

"Were the tennis-shoe prints found around where T.J. went down?"

"No, but there's a lot of grass in the area and the footprints wouldn't show up well there." The sheriff put his cowboy hat back on. "I understand you're hiring some guards for outside and bringing in dogs? I'll be back tomorrow to have a word with your son, Paul. In the meantime, I'm leaving a deputy out on the verandah."

"Yes, Sheriff Landon. Thanks for coming." T.J. escorted the trio to the door, then locked it behind them and pivoted toward his client, who was hanging back by the living room.

"If my son did this to you, I'll…" Paul's face fell, his coloring pale, his eyes haunted.

"Let's not speculate. Let's hear what he has to say."

"But he was trying to get away. Who else would have done it?"

"I don't know. But we need to assume the

person in Dallas did it. I'd rather think the worst-case scenario."

Paul laughed, no humor in the sound. "I think my son doing it is the worst-case scenario."

T.J. didn't say anything else. He'd rather deal with the teenager than an assailant moving freely around the ranch. If there was someone out there, T.J.'s appearance outside might have prevented Aaron from being kidnapped, which only reinforced the fact the dogs and guards were vital.

Ten minutes from the ranch, Aaron finally broke the silence in the car. "I didn't hit Mr. Davenport."

"You'll get a chance to tell him and your dad. But if you're right, then that probably means the stalker after your parents has been at the ranch and could be hiding somewhere there now."

"Why? They aren't doing their book tour anymore."

"The person's purpose may be more than

stopping the tour. Maybe he hates what your parents stand for or has some grudge against them."

"Then wouldn't they know that?"

"Not necessarily. Some people simmer until rage finally explodes in them."

Chloe crested a hill and saw the four-way stop sign at the bottom. She began to slow down, putting her foot on the brake. It went all the way to the floor and nothing happened. T.J.'s car picked up speed, careening down the incline.

NINE

"What are you doing? Slow down," Aaron shouted at Chloe.

Chloe gripped the steering wheel, pumping the pedal. "I can't. The brakes have gone out."

"What? Do something!"

She didn't see any headlights approaching the four-way stop, but she lay on her horn as she flew through the intersection. A stretch of level road with a shoulder gave her an idea. She drove off the highway and along the graveled edge as she pulled the emergency brake up.

The car came to a stop half off the pavement. Chloe leaned against the steering wheel, her hands still clasping it so hard, pain streaked up her arm.

Aaron collapsed forward, sucking in short,

shallow breaths. "We could have died. What if a car had been coming?"

"There wasn't one, and we're all right. That's what is important." Her hands shaking, she placed another call to the ranch.

When T.J. answered, he asked immediately without saying hello, "Where are you? I'll feel better when you get back here."

"I'm about six miles away on the highway going east about five hundred yards from the four-way stop sign. I didn't have a wreck, but I need someone to come pick up Aaron and me. The brakes gave out on your car."

"You had no warning?"

"No. It was sudden."

"Both sets of brakes failed?"

"Yep, back and front."

"I'll get someone to pick you up. I think I can catch the sheriff. I want a mechanic to check what caused them to fail at the same time."

With T.J.'s injury and the brakes going out in his car, it was obvious the assailant would go through the bodyguards to get to the couple.

* * *

T.J. came into the house through the front door and walked into the living room, where Mary, Paul and Chloe sat, discussing the addition of two dogs and several extra guards the day before. "The mechanic just delivered my car. Someone tampered with the physical linkage from the pedal to the brake master cylinder. I'm moving my Jeep into your three-car garage where we can protect it with your two vehicles. I don't want them sitting outside unattended. We don't need a repeat of last night." T.J. glanced around. "I thought Aaron was going to join you all."

"No, he's been holed up in his room on the phone a lot." Chloe shoved to her feet and began prowling the room. "Once we started talking about suspects, he was out of here. And I just came back from checking on him. It won't be as easy for him to try running away with the guards and dogs in the yard. That's why he took off two nights ago."

Mary stared out the window. "What a gray morning. The weather isn't helping my mood." She angled toward Paul next to her on the couch. "I'm not looking forward to going to Harrison's memorial service. What if something happens there?"

"It's outside in the park that he helped fund for the town. He was a good friend and he specifically asked for me to speak at his memorial service. I can't say no. His family is expecting me."

"After what happened in Dallas, I would think they would want us as far from the memorial service as possible."

Paul swallowed hard. "He was my best friend, and he passed away on his trip to Europe, his last hurrah before the cancer took him. I need to say goodbye to him."

"The sheriff and deputies will be there, as well as me and T.J. It's hard to hide something in an open field." Chloe leaned into the back of the lounge chair, grasping the top of the cushion.

"I'm just not myself lately. I'm tired, mentally and physically." Mary twisted her hands together in her lap.

Paul cupped them. "You should stay here with Chloe and the guards we hired. I'll feel better if you rest. We both don't need to be a target."

Mary blanched. "Don't say that."

"I've got an even better idea. You haven't had a chance to work in your greenhouse since we went on the speaking tour. I know there are things you need to do in there. Show Chloe some of the orchids you're growing."

"I can't do that. What will people—"

"We've never done things because of what people will think," Paul interrupted his wife. "Harrison wasn't your friend, but mine, and under the circumstances they'll understand."

Mary collapsed back against the couch. "I've been fretting about that since you reminded me of the memorial service yesterday. So much around here has changed. It's hard to take it all in."

Paul kissed her cheek. "Now you don't have to worry. You were supposed to work in the greenhouse yesterday, but then the day slipped by before you knew it."

Watching the married couple only reinforced T.J.'s desire to experience a relationship like what Paul and Mary had. That respect and understanding of each other was what he wanted, the same as what he'd seen when his parents were together.

His gaze skipped to Chloe observing the couple, too. Why hadn't it worked for them? Too young? They hadn't wanted to make that kind of commitment? Or was it fear? He'd known about Chloe's father being in the navy and always gone and the effect it had had on her mother. The type of job he and Chloe had chosen often caused them to be away from their home for weeks, possibly months, at a time. She wasn't exposed to two parents openly sharing their respect and love for each other like he had been, and yet he had hesitated, too, nine years ago. He should have come back to Dallas when Chloe's mother was better and persuaded Chloe to follow him to Washington. But then, that had been the first time he'd encountered a man he respected a lot and guarded dallying with a woman who wasn't his wife. Although not unusual for a person to have an affair, he hadn't thought the man he was assigned to was like that. His trust had been shaken and he'd never totally gotten it back.

"T.J."

He finally heard his name being called and dragged his focus away from what could have been. "Yes," he said to Chloe.

"When are you and Paul leaving?"

"In two hours. We'll probably be gone until four."

"You taking your car?"

"Yes, since the mechanic just finished working on it, I figure it's the safest car here at the ranch."

Paul snorted. "I never thought I would be sitting in on a conversation about a person being after me and one who would go to those lengths."

After talking with Aaron when he'd come back to the ranch, T.J. had been even more convinced whoever had targeted the Zimmermans on their tour had been here the other night and assaulted him. "You aren't the first person I've protected who has said that. Most people don't set out to make enemies."

"That doesn't comfort me." Paul shot to his feet. "I'll check on Aaron and let him know what I'm doing this afternoon, then I'll work on what I'm going to say at the memorial service. With all that's happened, I haven't had much chance."

T.J. watched Paul head up the stairs. Now that the windows were all hooked up to the alarm system, he could breathe a little easier concerning Aaron trying to leave again or someone getting into the house through a second-story window.

"For an active family, this all must seem like a prison. That's how Aaron feels." Chloe came up behind him.

Her presence—the sound of her voice—melted some of his tension. There were times he felt he had a whole household to protect, including Chloe. He didn't want anything to happen to her. He was responsible for her being here. What had happened when she'd driven his car had only strengthened that feeling. Yes, she was a good driver and a quick thinker. She didn't panic easily, but she and Aaron could have been seriously hurt that night—or killed. He shuddered at the thought.

She laid her hand on his shoulder, still slightly behind him. "You okay? All day yesterday you were quiet."

"I was supervising the changes in the alarm system and overseeing the new guards. You're a natural with the two German shepherds."

"Thanks. I've worked with dogs before. But I'm not letting you change the subject. You're upset about your car, aren't you?"

He pivoted. "What do you think? You could have been hurt."

"Or you, if you had been driving. The good news—I wasn't hurt and took care of the problem just fine. That night you were hurt, not me. You knew this could be a dangerous assignment. We're in a dangerous business. I was when I was a police officer. Every day I went to work, there was the potential of getting hurt."

"When I was younger, I thought of myself as invincible. I was trained well. I could deal with anything. Now I've seen how foolish those thoughts were. Nobody is invincible."

"But we have both been well trained. We're using our skills and abilities to help others." She slid her hand from his shoulder.

He missed her touch—more than he should. "Have you ever thought of giving it all up and doing something totally different?"

"Sure, I thought about doing something else. I seriously considered it a year ago when I was shot in the shoulder. I helped Kyra at the office for a while and liked that. But when I went back into the field, I fell right back into the groove, because I bring a sense of safety to people who need it. That's a good feeling. How about you? You quit the Secret Service, but you're still doing what you were doing for them—guarding people."

"It's crossed my mind, too. As I told you, I'm also looking at other options. Right now I feel unsettled."

"Our jobs don't help that. We're always

going from one job to the next in different places." She smiled, her green eyes sparkling. "We are who we are. We have to do what we think is best, what our purpose in God's plans is."

He stared into those glittering eyes and wanted to lose himself in them, to forget where they were for a few minutes at least. He wished they were anyplace but here in the middle of a case. He grazed his forefinger across her cheek. "It should have been me in my car," he whispered, trailing his touch to her chin as he leaned toward her and tilted up her head.

Her allure was too much to ignore anymore. His mouth caressed hers with feathery brushes before he drew her to him, his hands framing her face, his lips possessing hers with a deep kiss. For a moment, he allowed himself to focus totally on her. The house faded from his consciousness, and it was only Chloe and him together in their own private world.

Then a noise intruded on their interlude,

forcing T.J. to step away and swing his attention to Vickie coming down the hall from the kitchen.

"Where is everyone?" Mary's cousin asked as she crossed the foyer.

"Upstairs." T.J. wondered if Vickie had seen anything. From her expression, he didn't think so, but the incident confirmed in his mind he couldn't do that again. For a moment, he'd lost his awareness of his surroundings. Chloe consumed his focus, which in a dangerous situation wasn't wise.

"I came to tell y'all lunch is ready."

Chloe strode toward the staircase. "I'll let the family know."

She glanced at T.J. before proceeding to the second floor. Every part of her was aware of the man across the entry hall. His kiss had rocked her from the top of her head to the tip of her toes. It should never have happened. Yet she touched her lips and imagined it all over again. Warmth spread through her. She hated to think how flushed her cheeks were.

When Chloe started down the upstairs hallway, Paul came out of his bedroom, spied her and stopped. "Is something wrong?"

"No. I told Vickie I would let you all know lunch is ready."

He gestured toward a room down the corridor. "Mary is in our office. I'll get her."

"And I'll let Aaron know."

The teen had stayed in his room most of the time since he'd run away. When they had returned to the ranch, his face had been as white as the trim on the outside of the house. His eyes had still been dilated in fear. When he'd entered, he'd ignored everyone and raced up the stairs, his door slamming so loudly she wondered if the painting on the wall near his bedroom was still hanging up.

"No, find him," came from Aaron's room.

She paused and bent close to the wooden door. Was someone in there with him? Or was he on the phone? Either way he wasn't happy.

"Call me back. Soon." Sharpness hardened each word.

She knocked and waited. A minute passed, and she rapped again. If he didn't answer in five seconds—

Aaron swung his door open, a scowl etched into his features. But behind the expression she glimpsed something else. Fear? Worry? She hoped so, because both of those emotions would help keep him alive.

She peered around the teen and couldn't glimpse anyone else in his room. "Is there someone here?"

"Why do you ask?"

"Who is in this house is my business."

"No one is. I was on the phone. What do you want?"

"To talk," Chloe said, surprised at her words.

"What are you? Some kind of bodyguard/ therapist?"

She chuckled, trying to ease the tension vibrating from the teen. "Hardly. But I do know something about stress from a harrowing experience."

"I'm not..."

She looked him in the eye. "Scared?"

"Yeah. Brakes fail all the time. It was just an accident."

Since the teen hadn't joined the family much since the *accident,* he didn't know the brakes had been tampered with. T.J. had only just found out. Aaron needed to know the truth. "It wasn't an accident. Someone wanted the brakes to fail."

Aaron paled. His knuckles on the hand gripping the door whitened. He blinked, shook his head and said, "Then someone is after you and Mr. Davenport, not my parents."

"I wish that was the case, but that has been the car we've used to go places. It's okay to be worried about your parents, but they're in good hands. I know my job and will do my best to protect them and you." She stepped to the side to let him go first. "You coming downstairs for lunch?"

"No, I'm not hungry. I'll get something later."

While descending the stairs, Chloe couldn't

get the picture of Aaron out of her mind. He was angry and yet scared at the same time. She was so glad she wasn't a teenager. She could remember being angry with her dad for always being away. Most of the time she hadn't really felt she knew him. Did Aaron feel the same way about his parents?

Chloe sat back in her chair at the kitchen table. Paul and T.J. had left twenty minutes ago for the memorial service, and Vickie and Mary had cleaned up after lunch, then decided to have some hot tea. Chloe was a coffee drinker and declined the tea. Her thoughts kept straying to Aaron still in his room and Paul having to deliver a eulogy for a good friend while someone was after him.

"How have my orchids been doing in the greenhouse?" Mary sipped her tea in a china cup with tiny red roses.

"I'm not you, but I followed your watering instructions and none died," Vickie said with a laugh. "I'm surprised you didn't run out there the first chance you got when you came home."

"That speaks to how upset I've been. Until Paul mentioned them to me today, I'd forgotten about my orchids." She put her hands to her face and rubbed it, then turned to Chloe. "I've been raising orchids and showing them for years. My cousin has been gracious enough to fill in for me when I'm gone, but she's right. I always check on them when I get home. I didn't this time, and I can't believe it."

"That's what I said to Paul earlier this morning. I've been worried about you." Vickie rose and brought the pot of hot tea to the table and topped hers off. "Are you sure you wouldn't want any, Chloe?"

"Yes. I'm fine with water."

"Do you remember how we used to have tea parties all the time while we were growing up?" Vickie eased into her chair and sighed. "It's good to get off my feet."

Mary's forehead wrinkled with worry. "Is your gout bothering you again?"

"No. Thank goodness for that. It's just been a lot keeping up with all the people coming and going the past few days. Didn't the sheriff call right before Paul and T.J. went to town? Has Sheriff Landon discovered anything about who was here the other night and tampered with T.J.'s car?"

"Yes. He called. No evidence was found in T.J.'s car to point to who could have tampered with the brakes and hit T.J. over the head. All we know is someone knew what he was doing. But there was no guarantee the brakes would have failed at a certain time." Chloe sipped some water.

Vickie cocked her head. "So why do it?"

"There was a good chance it would have been driven with either Paul or Mary or both of them in the coming days. For instance, Paul's attending the memorial service. He was even going to come home in the middle of his speaking tour to do that. And where Paul goes, T.J. does, and he likes to drive his own car."

"Who in the world would do something

like that? I've known you all my life. You wouldn't hurt a fly." Vickie patted Mary's hand. "You're like a big sister to me. If your parents hadn't taken me in…" She blinked, and a tear rolled down her cheek. "I might have gone into foster care."

"No, you wouldn't. The family wouldn't have allowed that. You're part of the Benson family."

"I'm a third cousin."

"But still family. So that's that." This time, Mary patted Vickie's hand. "And just for the record, I'm only six weeks older than you."

Vickie laughed. "I always used to kid her that she was my elder. When she turned thirty and I gave her some antiaging cream, it became a running joke between us. She got me back when my birthday came up that year, although I think the walker was a bit much."

"Did you have any sisters or brothers?" Mary asked Chloe.

"No, just me. I always wanted a big sis."

"Not a younger one?" Mary finished the last swallow of her tea and pushed back her chair.

"Nope. I had a friend who had a younger sister who was a pest."

"I have a feeling I have a lot of work to do in the greenhouse so I think I'll head outside. It will be a good time for me to pray and think." Mary put her cup in the sink, grabbed her sweater and started for the back door.

"Wait a sec. Let me grab my jacket." Chloe rushed from the kitchen and took the steps two at a time. After retrieving her coat, she paused at Aaron's door and knocked again.

This time he answered right away. "I knew it was you. It's different from my mom or dad's knock."

"Just wanted to let you know your dad has left and your mom will be out in the greenhouse. It's all clear if you want to get something to eat."

He pulled himself up straight. "I'm not avoiding my parents."

"You aren't? You could have fooled me." Chloe hurried down the stairs and to the kitchen. When she entered and Mary was gone, she asked, "Did she go to the green-house alone?"

"Yes, I tried to stop her, but it's only ten feet from the back door."

It was hard to get clients to realize the normal freedom they had at their house had to be suspended completely while they were being protected. Even going out on their front porch could be problematic or dangerous.

Chloe stepped out onto the deck and headed for the greenhouse off to the side. Halfway there a scream coming from inside the glass building shuddered down her length. Her first instinct was to rush in. But caution stayed her actions. Through the window she couldn't see where Mary was. Chloe withdrew her gun and clasped the handle, then inched the door open, peering into the building.

Frozen, Mary stood against a post, her eyes wide with fright as she stared at an area under a table halfway down the middle row.

"Mary, what's wrong?"

She slowly rotated her head toward Chloe.

"A snake. Under the table." Then she returned her attention to where the reptile must be.

"What kind?"

"A rattler." Mary flinched when the snake began rattling its tail.

TEN

"It's going to get me again," Mary said in a high-pitched voice, frantically looking around the greenhouse as though searching for a place to hide.

"You've been bitten?"

"Yes, on my leg."

Chloe dropped her gaze and found where some blood seeped through Mary's cotton tan pants. "Can you move this way slowly?"

"No. It's looking at me. It's huge." Mary's voice rose with each word as hysteria took hold of the woman.

"Stay still. I'm going to try to kill it."

The rattling sound bombarded off the walls. Chloe gave the snake a wide berth to come up behind it and get a shot at it. She didn't have anything to kill the serpent with but her gun, and if Mary was bitten, she needed help immediately.

When Chloe eased closer, she locked on to a coiled greenish gray snake with diamonds down its back and its rattle shaking. A diamondback? She inched toward a place where she had a good view of the reptile, which had arched its back and brought up its head as though it would strike again.

Making sure she was clear of hitting Mary, Chloe aimed her Glock at the head and squeezed off a shot. She hit her target, and it collapsed to the floor, but the body twitched.

Chloe saw a shovel leaning against a wall and snatched it, then crept cautiously toward the rattler to make sure it was dead. Some animals moved after they were killed. She prayed that was the case with this snake.

When she approached the serpent, she brought the shovel down on the reptile right behind its head and cut it off. The body still jerked, but at least the rattler couldn't bite anymore. She shoved it as far away as she could, then turned her attention to Mary, who had slid down the post.

Her face etched in pain, Mary clasped the bite area on the calf of her leg.

"Take deep breaths. Calm down. Think of God holding you in His arms right now. I'm going to get some help."

The first call she placed was 911 to have a helicopter airlift Mary. She would need to be flown to the nearest hospital with a supply of antivenin. Then she called Vickie and asked her to bring soap and water with a cloth. Next, she called Zach and asked him to come to the greenhouse because Mary needed to be carried into the house. Last, she got hold of T.J.

"What kind of rattler?" he asked.

"I think a diamondback. There are diamonds down its back."

"Send me a picture. I'll show it around. When giving antivenin, the hospital will probably need to know exactly what kind of snake."

"Just a sec." Chloe took several pictures

from different angles and sent them to T.J.'s cell phone.

"Thanks. I'll give you a call when I find out anything."

"Where's Paul?"

"Speaking with the family. The memorial service is about to start. I'll grab him and we'll be there as soon as possible."

"The AirLIFE is coming from San Antonio, but you should be back before it arrives."

As Chloe hung up, Vickie came into the greenhouse, followed by an out-of-breath Zach.

"Where's Mary? Did she fall?"

Chloe hadn't gone into details with Zach or Vickie because that would delay Chloe from finishing all the calls she needed to make. And time was working against Mary. "A rattler bit her. Do you know much about that kind of thing?"

"Sure. I've been bitten by a diamondback here on the ranch, but it's cold right now. They aren't out at this time of year." His jaw clenched with that statement.

"Maybe he found his way in and made his home here."

"I guess it's possible." Zach knelt next to Mary. "Let me take a look. Vickie, wash the area, then put the cold cloth over it. We need to make sure you keep the wound lower than your heart." He glanced around and saw the snake. "I'll carry you to the house once Vickie cleans your injury."

"Thanks, y'all. I never expected to see a rattler in here in February. I know we've had some warm days, but it's cold most of the time."

Zach inspected the still-twitching snake. "Its reflexes will react long after it's dead. We'll need to carefully dispose of the head where the venom is. It's still as lethal even after death." Zach took out his phone and took several pictures. "I have a friend who is an expert on rattlers. I'm sending this to him and I'll call him once I get Mary inside and make sure he looks at it."

"It's not a diamondback?" Chloe stared at the dark diamonds on its back.

"I'm not sure, and you need to tell the doctor exactly what type of rattler." He lowered his voice and moved away from Mary. "She doesn't need to get excited. We need to keep her blood pressure down, if possible. There is a kind called the Mojave rattlesnake that looks like a diamondback, but its venom is different. It's a neurotoxin, very deadly if not treated correctly. The venom is much worse than other rattlesnakes. I think it's a Mojave one because the diamonds don't go all the way down its back. This rattler is a different color, too, but I may not be familiar with all the colors of a diamondback."

"I'm all done," Vickie said, and rose, her hands trembling.

As Zach lifted Mary, she winced. He trudged out of the greenhouse while Vickie ran ahead to open the back door. "I'm putting you in the living room on the couch." He looked at Chloe. "Are Paul and T.J. on their way back to the ranch?"

She nodded.

"I'll go and let Aaron know." Vickie began to mount the staircase.

"No." Chloe hurried toward Vickie and continued in a whisper. "I don't want him upset about his mother. It's important that she remains calm. After we leave, you can tell him and blame it on me."

"But—but…"

Chloe released Vickie but didn't go into the living room until Vickie descended to the foyer. "Tea. Get her some calming tea. The helicopter is probably twenty minutes out. And when it does land, please keep Aaron back if he hears it."

"I'll sit here on the bottom stairs after I get some tea for Mary."

Chloe went into the living room as Zach checked the bite, then stood back.

"Mary, I know it hurts like the dickens, but you'll be able to get the help you need. I'm calling my friend. Once we've accurately ID'd the type of rattler, the rest is a piece of cake."

"Really?" The creases in Mary's forehead emphasized her worry.

Chloe walked with Zach toward the entry hall. "Will you watch for Paul and T.J. and the helicopter?"

"Yes, and I'll find out what kind of snake it is. If my friend isn't sure, he'll know someone who will be. Rattlesnakes are common around here. But not the Mojave variety. They're only in the southwest corner by El Paso." He tipped his hat toward her. "Leave it to me."

As Zach left the house, Chloe sent a silent prayer to the Lord. Mary was in His hands now.

Back in the living room, Chloe pulled up a stool and sat beside Mary. "Okay?"

"I'm trying to be. Will you pray with me?"

Chloe held Mary's hands, cold and clammy, and bowed her head. "Father, I know Mary is in the best hands there are. Please give her the calmness she needs, knowing You are here for her. Pave the way for her to arrive at the hospital quickly and help there to be a fast response to her snakebite. Blanket her in Your love and assurances. Amen."

Carrying a mug, Vickie entered the room. "Here you go, Mary. A nice cup of tea. I know how much you like this flavor."

"Thank you. It's sweet you thought of that." Mary took the tea, her hands shaking.

Chloe wrapped her hands around Mary's and steadied the mug while her client brought it up to her mouth.

By the time Mary had drunk half her tea, the noise from a helicopter flying over the house flooded the room.

Mary pressed the mug into Chloe's hand. "Where's Paul?"

"They're coming as fast as they can."

A few minutes later, the front door banged open, and Paul rushed into the living room a few steps ahead of T.J. Chloe rose quickly to allow Paul to sit with Mary.

"Okay, hon?" Paul smiled, but Chloe could see the effort it took as his gaze latched on to the swelling leg.

"I'll be fine. Chloe has arranged everything. From that sound, the AirLIFE helicopter is here to take me to the hospital."

"I'm coming with you." Paul brushed Mary's hair back from her forehead, then wiped away the sweat that had popped out on her face.

Chloe exchanged glances with T.J. If there was only one spot, she needed to go. If the snake had been put into the greenhouse, what did the perpetrator have in store for Mary? He would know she would be flown to the nearest hospital that could treat her.

While T.J. held the front door open, Zach showed the AirLIFE medical team into the house with their gurney as he said, "The snake was a Mojave rattlesnake. I had it ID'd by a zookeeper I know."

"We'll notify the hospital so they have everything ready when we get there," the medic said as Paul moved back to let the team prepare Mary for transport.

"I'm coming with you. I have several photos of the snake I killed on my cell," Chloe said to the man in charge, noticing T.J. had stepped outside.

"Who are you? A relative?"

"No, I'm Mary's bodyguard, and she needs protection. There have been some attempts on her life. This being the most recent one."

The team leader swept his attention to Paul. "Are you the husband?"

"Yes, and she is right. Will you have room for me, too?"

T.J. came back into the house with Sheriff Landon as the man replied, "This is highly unusual."

"I'm the sheriff of this county, and Mary Zimmerman will need protection. Please do what you need to make it happen."

The team leader glanced from one person's face to the next, then said, "I'll take care of it. You both can come. Anyone else will have to drive." Then he gave the name of the hospital where Mary would be transported for emergency service.

Paul took Mary's hand as they wheeled her out of the house, sitting up on the gurney to keep her heart higher than her leg. All color was bleached from her face. She bowed her head and began murmuring a prayer.

As Chloe followed, T.J. walked beside her. "Where's Aaron?"

"About forty minutes ago when I checked last, he was in his room. He doesn't know. He was listening to his music using earphones, so he must not have heard the helicopter land."

"I'll bring him with me." T.J. squeezed her hand. "Take care."

Chloe stared down at the ranch as the helicopter took off. How had the snake gotten into the greenhouse in the dead of winter hundred of miles from its territory?

From the highway, the lights of San Antonio glittered in the dark up ahead. T.J. glanced at Aaron sitting still next to him in the front seat, staring out the windshield as he had most of the trip from the ranch. When T.J.'s cell phone rang, Aaron flinched but didn't look his way.

"T.J. here."

"We made it safely to the hospital. Mary is in the E.R. being treated. They gave her the antivenin for the Mojave rattlesnake.

They had to wait for it to be flown in from El Paso. Now it's wait and see. I'm seated outside Mary's room with Paul."

"How was she when she went into the room?"

"Feeling nauseated and having some problems breathing."

"Make sure Paul stays with you until I get there. I'm probably half an hour or so away." T.J. kept his attention shifting from the road to Aaron to the cars around them.

"How's Aaron holding up?"

"Okay. Vickie is staying at the ranch since we have those guards."

"See you in a while."

T.J. hung up. "Your mom has gotten the antivenin."

"Will she be all right?" The teen's voice quivered, as did his hands. He fisted them.

"Most people recover."

"Most?"

"Some arrive too late for the treatment to work."

"Did she?"

"I believe she arrived in time. We got her there as fast as we could."

Aaron sank back against the seat as though he'd released all the air from his lungs. "What's a rattlesnake doing in the greenhouse?"

"Good question. Chloe and I believe it was put there on purpose. That species of rattlesnake's range in the U.S. is southern California, Arizona, New Mexico and a small area in Texas's southwest corner. Not between Houston and San Antonio. Its habitat is desertlike land. Not to mention it's winter and has been too cold for snakes."

"Maybe it found its way in because the greenhouse is heated."

"I don't think so."

"The person after Mom and Dad came on the property and put the snake in there?" Fear shook Aaron's voice.

"A definite possibility. He could have put it in the greenhouse the evening you ran away, or the snake could have been there for a while. Your mother usually goes into the greenhouse several times a week, if not more. If he did it earlier, it was only a matter of time."

Aaron crossed his arms over his chest and lowered his head.

"We have to consider everything and prepare for the worst."

"Someone has been at our ranch," Aaron mumbled, keeping his chin down.

"Don't worry about it. Chloe and I will protect you and your parents. That's why it's important to follow our instructions. Your mom went out to the greenhouse without waiting for Chloe. We always like to check a place out before you go inside. That's also why it's important you don't go outside without one of us."

"I never meant this to happen. I…"

T.J. shot a look at Aaron. "What do you mean?"

The teen remained silent.

"Aaron?"

"I've wished my parents were regular people, not always in demand to speak and attending events. Everyone wants something from them. I've missed the time we were a normal family living on the ranch."

"They have an important message. They're trying to help others."

"Sometimes *I* need their help myself, but they're always unavailable. It didn't use to be that way." Aaron lifted his head and peered at T.J. "I've given up on getting any of their time."

"Since you've been back at the ranch, all you've wanted to do is return to school. You've got their undivided attention, and you stay in your room. Why?"

"They're there but not really. If they aren't on the phone, they're working in their office or..." Aaron shrugged. "What's the use? I *need* to get back to school. I belong there."

"We need to catch who is after your family first. I suggest making an effort with your parents when they return to the ranch. They're trying to fill their time so they don't think about what's happening around them."

Aaron harrumphed and turned to look out the side window.

Something wasn't right. Aaron wasn't telling him everything. Was it because of his emphasis on needing to get back to school? He'd said the same thing to Chloe when she'd picked him up on the highway to Houston. From what he'd gathered from Paul, Aaron's grades at Bethany Academy were passing, but that was all. Aaron used to love the ranch, according to Paul, had even talked about running it one day.

Fifteen minutes later, T.J. parked in the hospital's visitor lot. As they strolled toward the main entrance, T.J. placed a call to Chloe to see where they were now.

"Mary is still in the E.R. For sure she will be staying overnight. Beyond that will depend on how fast she starts to recover."

"We'll be there in a few minutes."

When T.J. and Aaron came into the emergency room, Paul spotted them and headed straight for his son. He enveloped Aaron in a hug. "You're safe."

The teen squirmed from Paul's arms. "But Mom isn't. You aren't. This is all happening because of you, Dad." Aaron stomped toward Chloe.

His son's words hurt Paul. T.J. could see it in the Paul's eyes as he fought to recover from what Aaron had said.

"This isn't your fault, Paul. The person doing everything is at fault. Don't let Aaron's frustration and anger convince you otherwise," T.J. said.

"Aaron and Mary have always been closer than he and I have been. I've tried. We don't seem to speak the same language. I thought the ranch would help us grow closer, but lately he's lost interest even in that."

"He's scared. I could tell by his tone in the car coming here. He's worried and struck out at the safest person—you."

The doctor came out of Mary's room in the E.R. Paul hurried back to him. T.J. followed, giving his client some space to talk privately with the man. When the doctor finished and left, Paul's shoulders lifted, then fell.

"Is Mary going to be all right?" T.J. said in a whisper, in case the news wasn't good.

Paul nodded, then turned toward Aaron and Chloe sitting across the hall. "They're moving her to a room for a couple of days if all goes well. She didn't have an allergic reaction to the antivenin and it seems to be working."

"Can I see Mom, then?"

"Yes, the doctor suggested we grab something to eat while they get her settled in her room."

Aaron pinched his lips together for a moment then said, "I'm not hungry. I'll stay and follow them up to the room."

"I think getting something to eat for dinner is a great suggestion, Aaron. I know your mom would want that. I'll stay with her and make sure nothing happens to her and see you all in a while." Chloe smiled at Aaron. "Do me a favor. Bring me a large cup of coffee. Okay?"

"I guess I can." The reluctance in Aaron voice carried over into his slow moves as he rose, his gaze straying to the room where his mother was. "We'll get to stay with her, won't we?"

"Yes. Let's go." Paul started to put his hand on his son's shoulder, but Aaron dodged the attempt.

T.J. stepped between the two. "I'm starved. I hope the food is half as good as Vickie's." He glanced back at Chloe. "Call and let me know which room."

"I will. You all let me know what is good or not."

As T.J. walked away from Chloe, he noticed what adrenaline had gotten her through the crisis was fading and weariness was beginning to set in. But he knew and trusted Chloe. No matter what, she would do the best she could to keep Mary safe.

Chloe sat on the small sofa in Mary's hospital room with Aaron pacing. Twenty-four hours had passed, and she was improving. The doctors were pleased with her progress.

"She sure has been sleeping a lot. I don't think the doctors are telling us everything."

Aaron kneaded his thumb into the palm of his hand.

"Her body is resting, which is the best thing she can do at this time," said Chloe.

Aaron walked to the door and peeped out into the hall, not for the first time since Paul and T.J. had left. "How long does it take for them to meet with the hospital? What if something happened? What if—"

"Aaron, it's only been twenty minutes. Working everything out concerning payment and insurance can take time. And besides, T.J. knows what he's doing. He worked for the Secret Service for years."

Aaron swept around, still working his thumb into his hand. "Who did he guard?"

"I know for quite some time he was on the vice president's detail, but there were other government officials he protected, too."

"Really?" For a moment Aaron's tense features relaxed, then a movement out of the corner of his eye caused him to pivot toward the bed.

Mary blinked several times. When she

finally fixed her gaze on her son, she attempted a smile. The corners of her mouth twitched, then the grin collapsed.

"Mom, you're awake. I've been worried about you."

Mary licked her lips and reached toward the plastic glass on the table near her.

Aaron rushed to her and picked it up, then helped her take a few sips.

"Thanks. I missed seeing you this morning."

"If I'd known you would wake up, I'd have waited to eat. Are you all right? Any pain?"

Is this the same angry teen from a few days ago?

"I'll be fine, Aaron. You don't need to worry about that. Worrying is a wasted emotion."

Chloe rose. "I'm going to give you two some time alone. I'll be outside the door if you need anything."

As the door swung closed, she heard Aaron say, "I didn't mean for this to happen to you.

I wanted us to have more time together, but not this way."

Could Aaron be responsible?

ELEVEN

For a few seconds in the hospital hallway, the thought rolled around in Chloe's mind, and yet while the attacks had been organized and planned out, Aaron had been at school. She and T.J. had been keeping an eye on the teen to make sure he didn't pull another stunt like he had the first night. So how could he have put a snake in the greenhouse? Although she couldn't totally dismiss the possibility Aaron was responsible, she wouldn't say anything to Mary or Paul unless she had proof. She would do some digging around and talk with Kyra and T.J.

The elevator at the end of the hall swished open, and T.J. and Paul exited it. T.J. smiled when he caught her gaze.

As they neared, Paul asked, "Is the doctor or nurse in there with Mary? Where's Aaron?"

"He's talking with his mom. He's been upset, and I gave them some time alone."

"Mary's up?"

"Yes. You should go in and spend some time with the two of them. Aaron has been struggling with this whole situation." T.J. grasped the handle. "I'll stay out here with Chloe."

"That's a great suggestion. We need to bond as a family again." Paul walked into the room as T.J. held the door open.

Chloe turned to T.J. "When I was leaving a few minutes ago, Aaron said something strange. The first thing he said to Mary was, *I didn't mean for this to happen to you.* Could he be involved in what is happening to his parents?"

"I don't know. We can never rule anything out. He's been very upset since the incident with the rattlesnake. I don't think he's acting. That doesn't sound like a guy who planned all of this."

"That's what I was thinking, but I'm going to have Kyra look into his friends and Bethany Academy."

"We shouldn't tell Paul and Mary. They have enough to deal with. Besides, I talked with your friend Rob. They discovered who leaked the information where the Zimmermans were staying in Dallas, which led to the reporter paying us an unorthodox visit that night—Nancy Carson."

Chloe blew a soft whistle. "The publicist. What was she thinking?"

"According to Matthews, Nancy was trying to stir up publicity for the Zimmermans. She was capitalizing on the pranks being pulled at their events. Her words, not mine. She was quite proud of her handiwork until the last stop and the fire. She told the police she knew nothing about the actual pranks and certainly not anything about the fire. She took a lie-detector test. I informed the publisher about what Nancy Carson had done and she is no longer the Zimmermans' publicist."

"You and I both know people can pass a

lie-detector test. That's why they aren't permissible in court as testimony."

"But she probably isn't behind what's happened at the ranch. She even canceled the interview the Zimmermans were going to have the morning after the fire. She didn't even complain."

"Mary has received a lot of publicity over this snakebite, so anything is possible. I won't rule her out until we discover who is doing this to the Zimmermans. Did Rob say anything about the cause of the fire?"

"Yes, the arson investigator ruled it arson. In fact, the police are looking for the woman Matthews carried out. After interviewing the man Paul and I helped out of the backstage area, it seems he had discovered the woman fleeing from the room where the fire was started. He stopped her and they ended up in a fight. She hit him over the head with something. As he went down, he grabbed on to her and took her down, too. That's the last he remembered before passing out."

Chloe thought back to the time Rob had

carried the woman out from behind the curtains. She'd never gotten a good look at her face. "All I can recall about her is curly long dark hair draping over Rob's arm with thick black framed glasses. Her head was turned away, but there was a big mole on her left cheek. I was too busy trying to get Mary out of the theater alive. You might ask Mary if she remembers anything about the woman, but she was so worried about you and Paul, her focus was on the stage."

"Matthews said when she arrived at the E.R., she left before the doctor could see her. She also gave a false name to the paramedics. He's going to work with the sketch artist for a picture. He'll send it to us."

"So the person after Mary and Paul could be a woman?"

"Or more than one person."

"I need to get some coffee. Maybe two or three cups."

"I'll come with you." T.J. kept his eye on Mary's room as they walked a few yards down the hall to the vending machine. "I also talked with Sheriff Landon about the snake investigation."

"Tell me he found the culprit." Chloe inserted her money and punched a button. Her cup plopped down and her coffee squirted into it.

"I wish I could. In one sense, a culprit was caught, chopped in half, even."

As she slid her cup out, she glanced at T.J. "Quit teasing me. I'm sleep deprived."

His eyes softened. "I'm sorry. I shouldn't dangle the carrot in your face."

She gave him a mocking frown. "I'm not a rabbit you're trying to lure into a trap."

He chuckled. "I'd never think that of you." His gaze bound to hers. "Ever." He started back toward Mary's room.

She couldn't shake the feeling of being cherished. Boy, she must really be sleep deprived if she was thinking that. "'Fess up. What are you holding back?"

He lounged against the wall next to the door into Mary's room. "After we left, Shane, Zach and the sheriff searched the greenhouse.

They couldn't find how the snake got inside if it supposedly crawled in, but Shane did find another one in the back by the orchid supplies. It wasn't happy to be disturbed, but the cowhand got him out without being bit."

At the thought there was another deadly rattler in the greenhouse, her knees went weak, and she leaned back next to T.J. "So there were two snakes. I guess whoever put the rattlesnakes in there wanted to make sure Mary got bitten. Did I ever tell you I hate snakes?" She sipped her coffee, her hand quivering.

T.J. grasped it, steadying the cup. "It's surprising what we can do because of our training when it's necessary."

"Yeah, but it doesn't stop the reaction afterward. The whole time I was in the helicopter I kept replaying those fifteen minutes in my mind. I knew if I'd missed hitting the rattler, it might strike Mary again, or me." Taking another drink of her coffee, she angled toward T.J. "God was looking out for us."

"Through this whole assignment I've felt that. I find I've been turning to the Lord more and more. I think that's your influence. You have reminded me how important putting my trust in the Lord is. For so long, my distrust was there under the surface, ready to rise at a second's notice."

She nodded once. "I'm glad to be of help. I know I've been trained well to do what I do, but there are just times all I can do is rely on Him."

"And yet you fear snakes." A grin tugged at the corners of his mouth, and a sparkle danced in his eyes.

"I suppose you have no fears."

"I wish that were the case. Sadly I do. Spiders."

"Spiders!" She pressed her lips together to keep from laughing. "Most of them are small, no more than your thumbnail."

"Not all of them. I know it's irrational to feel that way, but I have ever since I was a kid and I found a tarantula in my cabin at camp. It was huge." His eyes widened. "And I was small. My first time to go to camp. It bit me."

"A tarantula isn't poisonous."

"But I had an allergic reaction to its bite. I ended up in the E.R. the next day and went home from camp early. Needless to say, I didn't go again."

"Okay. I'm not going to laugh." But Chloe couldn't contain the smile that demanded its release.

"Let's just agree you'll take care of any spiders we encounter and I'll deal with the snakes."

She stuck her hand out. "A deal."

He closed his around hers but didn't shake it. He inched closer. "You know, I used to think I knew you well, but I didn't know that tidbit. What else about you are you keeping a secret?"

She chuckled, a bit shakily as the warmth from his touch spread through her. "It wasn't a secret. It never came up. Believe me, if I had seen a snake when we were dating, you would have known how I felt."

"I'm even more impressed by how you handled the situation yesterday."

Her pulse rate increased. Her breaths shortened. She wished they weren't in a hospital guarding three clients. She wanted him to kiss her again. Could they work out the second time around? What kind of relationship could they have when they both were on the road so much? Seeing Mary and Paul, who worked so well as a couple, she wanted that. They had problems, but they dealt with them together—that was one of their themes in their books. Working together to solve what was wrong. This was the first time she'd had a partner as a bodyguard, and although it was different and she'd needed to get used to the idea, it had worked well so far. Was that because it was T.J.?

"Do you think we've given them enough alone time?" Chloe finally asked, needing to remind herself that she and T.J. were still working.

"Probably not, but it's getting close to dinner." T.J. waved at the dinner cart coming down the hall for the patients. "We need to make some decisions about what we'll do this evening for food and rest. I think you need to go back to the hotel and catch some sleep before you stay tonight."

"Good suggestion."

T.J. pushed open the door, and Chloe went into the room first. Mary, Paul and Aaron had their heads bowed and their hands intertwined as Paul finished up a prayer. The scene gave Chloe hope everything would work out for the couple and their son.

Mary, who was sitting beside Chloe in the backseat of T.J.'s car late the next day, sighed loudly. "I'm so glad to be back at the ranch."

Paul, on the other side of Mary, clasped her hand. "I never want to see you in a helicopter again."

Mary smiled at him. "Me, either, and I hardly remember the journey."

Chloe's throat tightened at the love gushing from the two. The evening before had been a shift in the couple's relationship with Aaron. Their son had even participated in the conversation. She'd seen some of it before she'd gone to the hotel to shower and take a nap.

Another thing she liked about T.J. He seemed to know what she needed before she did. The rest had rejuvenated her.

When the car came to a stop in front of the house, T.J. climbed out first, slowly scanned the landscape and approached the guard with one of the dogs. They talked for a few minutes before T.J. made his way to the car and opened the back door for Chloe, then went around to the other side to let the Zimmermans out.

Chloe stood, doing her own survey of the ranch. In the distance she spotted Zach working on a pickup while two cowhands repaired the fence a couple of hundred yards away. The late-winter day was unseasonably warm, which made for a great one to spend outside. She wouldn't be surprised if Aaron wanted to go riding. She'd like to.

Aaron was first through the entrance and headed up the stairs, announcing he had some friends he needed to call.

When Mary walked into her home, Vickie

engulfed her in a hug. "I was so worried about you."

Mary leaned back. "What is that smell?"

"Your favorite dish, beef stew. I thought we would celebrate your safe return." Vickie rotated toward the living room. "Shane's been helping me decorate a little."

Mary strolled to the entrance and gasped. "Y'all did this for me?"

The room was filled with balloons and vases of flowers. Above the mantle hung a big sign with Welcome Back, Mary written across it. Mary glanced at her husband, tears shining in her eyes.

Paul shook his head. "I didn't have anything to do with this. It was all Vickie's idea. She wanted to surprise you."

"You shouldn't have."

"I had to do something," Vickie said. "You didn't want flowers or anything in your hospital room."

"I was only there a short time."

Chloe almost laughed out loud, because by the time they had left a few hours ago, the hospital room had been overflowing with flowers and potted plants from different people who had read about what happened to Mary. Finally, after the first twelve hours, Chloe had had the nurse's aide take what was delivered and pass them out to other patients.

Vickie waved toward the living room. "The balloons and sign are from me, but the flowers are from people in town."

Shane tipped his head. "Ranch hands and I have done a thorough search of the house, greenhouse, garage and any other place you might go to make sure there aren't any more surprises for you, ma'am."

Mary blushed. "Thank you, but really, all this fuss isn't necessary."

Paul came to Mary and clasped her upper arms from behind. "I know Chloe and T.J. didn't want a lot of people coming to the ranch, but tomorrow at church be prepared to be smothered with love. They have planned a celebration for you."

Chloe tensed. On the drive from San Antonio, Paul had insisted they would all go to church and give the Lord thanks for Mary's quick recovery. No matter what protest T.J. had thrown at the man, he had insisted they would be all right there. No one was going to keep him from being in God's house. They had a lot to celebrate. Mary was alive. Chloe had to agree with Paul, although it made T.J.'s and her job more difficult.

Shane started for the foyer. Vickie walked with him to lock the door after he left. The cowhand leaned down and gave the house-keeper a quick kiss on the cheek. Vickie's cheeks flushed a deeper shade of red than her cousin's had earlier.

When Vickie rejoined the group, Mary grinned. "Are you dating Shane?"

Vickie lowered her head and fiddled with her apron, smoothing it over and over. "He's sweet on the sweets I bake for the ranch hands a couple of times a week."

"That's wonderful. You should invite him to have dinner with us some time when everything isn't so up in the air."

"Oh, that does remind me. Sheriff Landon

is coming by later. I took it upon myself to invite him to dinner. He and his deputies combed the ranch, but couldn't find anything to indicate who had tampered with T.J.'s car or put the snakes in the greenhouse."

"Before all the festivities begin, I'm going to rest or I'll fall asleep at the dining room table." Mary crossed to the staircase with Paul close behind her, carrying the bag T.J. and Aaron had brought to San Antonio for the family.

Vickie scurried toward the back of the house, leaving T.J. and Chloe alone in the entrance to the living room. Chloe felt T.J.'s gaze on her and shifted to look at him. "We need to check the interior and exterior of the house."

"Definitely. A lot could be changed in two days. I'll talk with the guard outside and walk around the house, then I'll go down and talk with Zach and make sure the shed is still locked. It's not as big a deal now that the up-stairs windows are wired into the security system, but the harder we can make it for someone to get inside, the better."

"I'll go through the house and talk with Vickie. See if anyone came by the house. She does the ranch accounts for Mary and Paul. Could this have to do with the ranch, not their books and stand on certain issues?"

"Not a bad idea. I'll talk with Zach. I saw him earlier at the barn."

"I just want to make sure we're looking at this from all the different angles. At first it looked like someone wanted to stop the speaking tour. Now I don't know."

T.J. invaded her personal space, and usually when someone did that, it set off alarm bells clanging in her mind. But not this time. When they had worked together years ago, they hadn't been on equal footing. He'd been in charge of the task force trying to bring down a counterfeiting ring. Technically he was the lead on this assignment, too, but in reality they were partners. He'd gone out of his way to always consult her and get her input. How would she feel if he became her boss? Their dynamics might change yet again.

His gaze dropped to her mouth for a long moment, then lifted to her eyes, his look heart-melting. "I'll be glad when this is over. We have a lot we need to talk about when we don't have all these distractions."

Her heart rate kicked up a notch. Thinking about a possible future with T.J. made her realize she was falling in love with him again. And yet she'd loved him nine years ago, and it hadn't worked out.

T.J. passed the ranch pickup Zach had been repairing. The open hood stood up, and a toolbox was still sitting next to it on the ground. T.J. strode into the barn and headed for Zach's office to the left.

"The check is in the mail. If you don't receive it in a few days, call me back," Zach said, the sound of the phone slamming down echoed through the cavernous interior.

A cowhand at the other end glanced toward

the office, then went back to moving some hay bales.

T.J. stuck his head through the doorway. "Having trouble?"

"The feed company. They're insisting they haven't received the check for last month's bill. I saw Vickie write it and put it into an envelope to be mailed. I guess I'll have her stop payment on it and reissue the check if they don't get it in a few days. I don't like this new company, but Paul wanted to help them." Anger infused the foreman's voice.

"Are there problems at the ranch?"

"Don't get me wrong. Paul is great to work for, but when he tries to run the ranch, things happen. He's good at what he does, and I'm good at what I do. He usually gets territorial about this time every year. With spring approaching, we get very busy."

"And you don't have time to babysit?" T.J. cushioned his shoulder against the door frame, his arms folded over his chest.

"Exactly. Although I guess it isn't exactly

the same. You must know what it feels like. Your job is kinda like babysitting someone."

"Except the stakes are a lot higher." T.J. jerked his thumb to the left. "What's wrong with the pickup outside?"

"Sluggish and knocking."

"Do you work on all the vehicles for the ranch? I wouldn't think that would be part of your job description."

"I do sometimes. Also Willie or Shane. It's kinda nice as a change of pace." Zach stretched his arms above his head. "Office work is not my favorite part of the job. I appreciate it when Vickie comes down and sometimes helps out. Is Mary really all right? I've missed Vickie not being able to help the past week or so."

"Yes. It will take a while to be back to her old self, but she should be soon."

Zach rose. "Is there a reason you came to see me?"

"Not particularly. I was just trying to understand the ranch operations, and if there would be any reason for someone to be after the Zimmermans because of the ranch. I'm not so sure what's been happening is connected to Paul and Mary's books and campaign to make a change."

Zach blew a long, low whistle. "Paul and Mary pay good money for their help. They're fair, and I can't see one of my men upset with him. I'm usually the one who fires a ranch hand, after checking with Paul. So if someone had a beef, it would be with me."

"Have you fired anyone recently?"

"One, a month ago for continually smoking on the job."

"Smoking?"

"It's not allowed at the ranch, especially around the stable and barn. This area has been going through a drought off and on for a while."

"Who was the man?"

"Bo Moore." Zach came around his desk.

"Do you know where he went?"

"He lives in town. I wouldn't have given him a second chance when I caught him the first time, but Paul believes in second chances. I'm not as tolerant as Paul. And sure enough, I found him smoking again right outside the back door of the barn." Zach gestured in that direction.

T.J. pushed away from the doorjamb and moved out into the barn. "If you can think of anyone else, I'd appreciate if you'd tell me, no matter how small the reason. I've been surprised at some people's motivations. But usually it revolves around love/hate or greed."

When he exited the barn, a horse in the pasture across from the barn neighed. A light breeze blew from the south, the air warmer than it had been the past week.

T.J. took a couple of steps, stopped and turned back to Zach. "Have you replaced Bo Moore yet?"

"Actually, about a week before y'all came to the ranch."

"Where is the ranch hand?"

Zach frowned. "You're thinking the person could be my new guy?"

T.J. shrugged, not wanting to commit either way. "I suspect everyone."

Zach pointed to his chest. "Even me?"

"Yes."

The foreman's expression darkened. "Well, I'm not. Dave Cutter is repairing the fences in the far pastures. That's been his main job since he started. He couldn't have done the prank with the stink bombs because that was when he arrived at the ranch. He interviewed a few days before. He had excellent references. I don't hire just anyone."

"I'd appreciate talking with Dave Cutter when he comes in from working today."

"I'll send him up to the house."

"No. Call me and I'll come down here."

Without saying another word, Zach went back to work on the pickup. T.J. strolled toward the house. When he'd first come to the ranch, he hadn't thought it might be someone who worked at the place, although he'd had Kyra start a background check on everyone, especially the ones who were in contact with Paul and Mary. Even though Kyra hadn't alerted him to an anomaly in an employee's background, he knew that would take time to uncover. Now he didn't know if the attacks were connected to Paul and Mary's speaking tour and their message. But he would check in with her and add Bo Moore to the list.

When Sheriff Landon arrived at the front gate, Chloe accompanied T.J. out onto the verandah to wait for him to pull up to the house.

Chloe waved at the guard who passed with the dog. "How's Kyra coming with the background checks on the employees?"

"So far Zach, Vickie, Shane and Willie have checked out—at least their references. Nothing in their background was a red flag. She's going to look into Dave Cutter and Bo Moore for me next before completing the list of the rest of the ranch hands."

"Have you noticed the interaction between Shane and Vickie? I think she's sweet on him, and he returns the feelings. When you were down at the barn, he came up to the back door with some lame excuse he was making sure Vickie didn't need any more help setting up for the party for Mary tonight. Vickie blushes every time I've seen them together."

The corners of T.J.'s eyes crinkled. "Love must be in the air."

"No comment," Chloe said with a laugh and pretended a great interest in the sheriff's SUV approaching.

T.J. shook hands with the man first, then Chloe did. "I didn't want to talk about this in the house. Did you talk with Bo Moore?"

"Yep, and he has an alibi at least for the tampering with your car. He was gone to his brother's in Phoenix at that time. In fact, he found a job there and was boxing up his stuff to move soon. He didn't appear to have any hard feelings toward the Zimmermans or Zach. He was excited about the job he found in Arizona working on a dude ranch in the northern part of the state." Sheriff Landon rubbed the stubble of his beard. "In my opinion, he didn't do it."

"I respect your opinion. When's he moving?"

"In a few days."

"That sounds like good news to celebrate along with Mary's recovery," Chloe said. "We'd better head inside or they'll be wondering what is keeping us." She started for the front door when T.J.'s cell phone rang.

While he answered it, she escorted the sheriff inside and to the living room. Then, staying back by the entrance, she waited for T.J. to come inside. When he did, a scowl grooved his face.

She met him halfway across the foyer. "What's wrong?"

"That was Zach. Remember I said he was going to let me know when the new employee came back to the barn? He never did, and Zach went out to the area where he was supposed to be repairing the fence. The wood, barbed wire and tools were there, but not a sign of Dave Cutter. When Zach returned to the barn and checked where the ranch hand parked, the guy's car was gone."

TWELVE

"Kyra is tracking down the references that Zach checked for Dave Cutter, and so far she hasn't been able to get in touch with the first one. She'll call me when she gets something. What did Sheriff Landon say?" Chloe asked later that night when the celebration for Mary's homecoming was winding down.

T.J. sidled closer to Chloe, standing in the entrance to the living room, and lowered his head to whisper, "He's checking for a driver's license photo so we have a picture of him, but the deputy that went by the man's address said he wasn't there. The owner of the property isn't there, either. He's renting a garage apartment. Hopefully one of them will come home soon."

"For the first time, I feel we might be getting closer to what is going on. Look at Mary. She's trying to be the gracious hostess, but this has taken its toll on her." Chloe noted the dark circles and puffy eyes that Mary had tried to disguise with makeup.

Sitting on the couch, Paul cupped his wife's hand and put one arm around her shoulder as though he was trying to shelter her. "As much as you've enjoyed this little celebration, Mary, I think it's time you consider going to bed."

Mary looked at Aaron, then Vickie, before her attention skipped to Sheriff Landon and finally settled on Zach. "Thanks, y'all. This has touched my heart, and I wish I could stay up, but Paul's right."

Her husband grinned, his eyes lighting up. "You heard it. Mary has said I'm right. I want you all to remember that."

The sound of laughter sprinkled the air, but beneath it was the unspoken threat that still existed for the Zimmermans. Everyone quickly sobered. Zach and Sheriff Landon rose almost simultaneously.

Zach reached for his cowboy hat. "Ma'am, glad to see you're all right."

As the party broke up, T.J. walked with the sheriff and Zach toward the front door to let them out, then lock up and arm the alarm system.

Paul paused next to Chloe. "I'm seeing Mary to bed, then I need to talk to you and T.J. about tomorrow."

Aaron followed his parents upstairs while Vickie made her way to the kitchen.

"I'll take the right side of the house. You the left," Chloe said to T.J., and rotated toward the right to begin her perimeter check of the first floor.

With all windows and outside doors locked, she returned to the foyer to find T.J. talking with Paul.

He crossed his arms. "Mary and I don't want Aaron or Vickie to go to the event at our church."

"Too bad," Vickie said to Paul as she came into the entry hall. "I'm going. I agreed to not go to the store and sent Zach for the items

I needed, but I'm determined to be part of the church celebration. I'm getting claustrophobic. I need to get out of here. Besides, you don't know if the person is after me. I'm not part of the immediate family." Lifting her chin, she fixed her hard stare on Paul. "I agree Aaron should stay away."

For a long moment, Paul and Vickie exchanged looks before his mouth set in a frown. "Fine."

"Good night." Vickie ascended the stairs to the second floor.

"I personally wish you all would stay here," T.J. said in a steely voice, as if that would make a difference.

"Not an option. Mary and I are determined to make a statement that we are not afraid. We aren't stupid and will take precautions, but we won't be prisoners, either. Right now our lives are revolving around this madman."

"Does Aaron know?" Chloe asked, imagining the teenager's reaction. He'd shared the same thoughts as Paul on a number of occasions.

"No, but I'll tell him tomorrow morning. I do want an extra guard on duty in the house while we're gone."

His frown carving deeper lines into his face, T.J. nodded. "I'll see to it. The sheriff told me earlier he'd have deputies at the church."

Paul attempted a smile that failed. "I know how you feel about this, and if this wasn't for Mary, I would insist she stay home. Actually, I tried, but she wouldn't listen to me. It's become very important to her to show whoever is doing this that she's not afraid. I don't want to lose her, but she's right. If our message is to take back America, which means everyone fighting for what they believe in, I can't tell her not to go." He heaved a deep breath, then released it slowly. "I'd better go to bed, too. It's going to be a long day."

When Paul disappeared down the upstairs hallway, T.J. plowed his fingers through his hair and massaged his neck. "I want to shake some sense into Paul and Mary."

"We've guarded other clients who still went about their jobs. We can do this."

"I know we'll do the best we can, but ultimately if someone wants to get to them, he could, especially if he didn't care if he was caught."

"I don't think that's the case here. The guy is bold, but he's gone to a great deal of trouble to keep himself hidden."

"Don't forget the woman in Dallas at the last stop. She's still missing and could be involved."

"If the woman is involved, then there is more than one person. Whoever it is seems to enjoy messing with Mary and Paul."

"Maybe it's Dave Cutter and the police will find him."

"So you've decided—"

T.J. laid two fingers on her lips. "Shh. No more speculation tonight. It's not really our job. Our job is to be alert and keep our clients alive, although it would be nice if we could solve it so the Zimmermans have their life back." He took her hand and tugged her toward the stairs. "Let's sit and enjoy each other's company until everyone has gone to sleep. Tonight's my turn to sleep on the couch in the living room."

"But you did it the last time we were here."

"And you spent two nights with Mary in the hospital. I owe you a bed to sleep in."

"I imagine we're both light sleepers no matter where we lay our heads."

"True. That seems to come with the job." A smile slid across his mouth and spread to encompass his whole face, forming deep crinkles at the corners of his sparkling eyes. He was totally focused on her.

Tension slipped from her shoulders, easing the tightness there. "Have you ever wondered what would have happened to us if I had moved to Washington all those years ago?"

"Yes. Have you?"

"Of course. For months after you left. And again recently."

"And?"

She stared at the front door, knowing in her

heart she needed more than what her mom had had with her dad. "We wouldn't have worked out."

He touched her chin and turned her head toward him. "I agree. We needed different things from a relationship. Although I'm not a navy guy like your dad, I needed a port in a storm and you needed an anchor."

Surprised flittered through Chloe. "Exactly, but I haven't changed. How about you?"

"I don't know. My life has been in a bit of turmoil lately with me quitting the Secret Service and coming to live in Dallas. Working in the field gives me satisfaction that I'm doing something to make a person's life better or at least safer."

"Why did you pick Dallas?"

"It was familiar. I like the area. I wanted to be based in a large town with good airline connections to make it easy to travel."

"Did I figure into the decision?" She held her breath, the seconds ticking by slowly.

Finally he hooked an errant strand of her hair behind her ear. "It crossed my mind."

"I've been wondering about that." She smiled, more stress melting away. So much had happened since they'd become partners and, yes, they hadn't seen each other for years, but T.J. was still the same person deep down. Although she'd stated she had changed, she was also the same. She wanted the same things: something more than she had, something she'd been looking for. She'd decided T.J. wasn't that something nine years ago, but now she wondered if she'd been wrong.

He angled toward her, taking her hands in his. His look wiped away the time they had been apart, and she felt whisked back to when they had been dating. He cupped her face, the feel of his roughened fingers caressing her cheek sent shivers down her spine. "I wish we were somewhere else."

He bent close to her, his breath whispering against her lips. Goose bumps rose on her arms. Then his mouth connected with hers in a kiss that removed the last vestige of tension. All her senses homed in on T.J. as he deepened the kiss.

Someone coughed at the top of the stairs. T.J. pulled back at the same time she did.

Aaron descended, a smug expression on his face. "Sorry I interrupted you. Going to the kitchen to get a snack." He continued his path toward the back of the house.

"I'm sure we'll hear about that tomorrow." Chloe tamped down the sensations rampaging through her. She'd wanted that kiss more than she had realized.

T.J. straightened, putting more distance between them on the step. "Probably. Which brings me to another decision I have made. Working with you isn't a good idea. You're a distraction, as a moment ago illustrated. No matter what I do or say, I've found myself thinking on occasion of you when the Zimmermans should be paramount in my thoughts."

Even though they worked well as a team, she had to admit the same thing. This was neither the time nor the place. "Should Kyra send someone else to replace me?" Although she knew where he was coming from, the idea she would be replaced with another bodyguard bothered her.

Leaning forward, he settled his elbows on his thighs and clasped his hands, his head averted. "We'll talk about it after tomorrow. But if I had to make a decision tonight, I would say no, because we do work so well together. I know the Zimmermans wouldn't like it. We're professionals. We know how to suppress our emotions when we need to." He rose and put some space between them. "We have so little downtime when we're on a job. It's hard not to touch you, relax, enjoy getting to know you all over again when we do have a moment for ourselves."

As he said those words, she could see a neutral expression descend over his features, as though the kiss had never happened. His hands, which were at his sides, opened and closed.

Chloe pushed to her feet, weariness blanketing her. She couldn't shut down her emotions as easily, but she had to. Being in this profession wasn't conducive to a relationship.

Adam had taught her that. And right now this was her livelihood, and she intended to do the best job she could.

"I'll check the second floor before going to bed. See you in the morning."

As she climbed the stairs, his gaze bored into her. She felt it deep in her heart. She refused to look back. She was better off by herself rather than with a man married to his work. *Nine years ago he was, and now he still is.*

The next day after the event at the Zimmermans' church, T.J. pulled up to the entrance of the ranch, releasing his tight grip on the steering wheel to push the button for the gate to open. Slowly—too slowly for him—they swung wide, and he drove through, heading toward the house. Although the event at the church had gone without a problem, he wouldn't breathe easy until Paul, Mary and Vickie were inside their home.

"Does everyone still have their bulletproof vest on?" Using the rearview mirror, T.J.

looked at Vickie and Mary to make sure, because the two women had complained about the awkwardness of wearing it.

"Yes, we do," Mary said, twisting her mouth into a thoughtful expression. "How in the world do the police wear these all the time? It's uncomfortable. The sheriff can have this back gladly."

"It depends on the officer and the situation." A chuckle accompanied Chloe's words.

T.J. wished they had agreed to wear them into the church, but when the sheriff had offered them to the Zimmermans, they'd drawn the line at walking into the celebration in bulletproof vests. So T.J. had pulled up to the back door within several feet so his clients hadn't had far to go. Then Chloe had rushed them inside.

When T.J. stopped in front of the antebellum home, he started counting down the minutes until the Zimmermans were safe.

"See, nothing happened," Mary said with a long sigh. "It was good to see everyone. A lot of people are praying for us."

"Stay in the car until Chloe and I come around and open the door. Hurry inside. Chit-chatting can take place in the house."

"At least we're home safely," Vicky said with a shaky laugh.

T.J. climbed from the vehicle at the same time as Chloe did. Surveying the area, he skirted the front of the car while Chloe went around the rear. As he reached toward the handle, his gaze snagged Chloe's. He tipped his head, and then opened the door.

Paul rose quickly and started to help Vickie and Mary out, but T.J. ushered him toward the house. "Chloe will take care of them."

A cracking sound split the air, and the column splintered inches from Paul's head. The second T.J. heard the noise he tackled Paul to the ground, the car partially shielding them.

Another bullet hit the concrete step not covered by the Jeep. T.J. pushed Paul until the car blocked him.

"Get down." As T.J. drew his gun, he swung his attention to the women. Mary was still inside the car hunkered down while Vickie and Chloe used the Jeep as protection.

The two guards let their dogs go while one man ducked behind the verandah and the other used a tree as a shield.

The front door banged open, and Aaron ran outside waving his arms and shouting, "Stop! Stop! You aren't supposed to do this."

T.J. ran low toward the teen and barreled into him, sending them both flying into the house. T.J. hit the tile floor and rolled the kid out of view. "Stay down. Don't move." Then he crept toward the door and peeked out. "Okay, everyone?"

"We're all right," Chloe answered.

T.J. called 911, then shouted out the door, "Help is on the way." He hoped whoever was firing on them would hear and try to make his getaway.

The guard behind the tree zigzagged toward the pecan grove across the drive.

When there weren't any more shots, T.J. rotated toward Aaron. "Stay." Then he headed outside at the same time the guard by the verandah moved forward and the second one near the paved drive ran across the road and took cover behind a tree.

"Get them in the house one at a time when I give you the go-ahead," T.J. said to Chloe as he passed her.

Scanning the trees, T.J. quickened his pace and plunged into the thick woods directly across from the house. Pecans, not gathered last fall, crunched beneath his feet, making moving harder.

The sound of the dogs' barking grew louder, and then a shot went off, followed by a yelp.

Shielding Vickie, Chloe hurried her toward the front door, then came back for Mary, all the while keeping vigilance on the pecan grove across the drive. She spied T.J. vanishing in the thick of the vegetation.

Paul helped Mary out of the back, his wife's face the pasty white that Chloe had seen when the snake had bit her. She took Mary's arm. "Run as fast as you can."

As Mary straightened, she froze when she

heard the noise: the gunning of an engine coupled with a dog yelping echoed through the stand of trees.

"Go. Now." Chloe pushed her forward to get her to move. Again she used her body to protect Mary.

When she was safe inside, Chloe came back for Paul, who was already part of the way to the house. Frowning, she fell into step behind him.

More gunfire blasted the air as Chloe slammed the front door closed and locked it. "Sit on the stairs." Then she took up watch, using the window in the living room. Every ten seconds or so, she glanced at the family huddled together on the bottom couple of steps.

She saw no movement in the pecan grove. *Please be all right, T.J.*

When T.J. saw one German shepherd down by an oak, he waved to the nearest guard a few steps behind him. "See to him."

Near the highway about four hundred yards

from the front lawn of the house, T.J. spied the back of a red pickup pulling away and squeezed off a couple of shots, knowing the low probability of him hitting one of the tires. As T.J. jogged to the road, the other dog gave chase after the old Chevy truck without a license plate. When the vehicle had disappeared around a curve, T.J. whistled for the dog to return. The black-and-tan German shepherd loped toward him, his tongue hanging out the side of his mouth.

T.J. patted him on the head and rubbed his back. "Good boy. Let's return to the house after we check on your buddy."

When he arrived where the other dog had gone down, the guard already had the animal in his arms and was starting back toward the house. Over his shoulder he said, "There's some material with some blood on it by where Rover was. I think he bit the shooter."

"How's Rover?" T.J. squatted by the trunk.

"He should be okay once the vet patches him up."

A piece of tan cotton, possibly from pants, with red drops on it lay on the ground. Was the blood from the assailant or the dog? That would be easy enough to discover, and this could be good evidence to help convict the shooter.

Paul had been inches away from being shot in the head. The assailant had gone for the head when the chest area was an easier and bigger target—he must have somehow known Paul was wearing a bulletproof vest under his coat. Something to mull over.

T.J. left the cloth to be processed by the sheriff's office. Straightening, he weaved his way through the pecan trees and dense brush beneath them. When he reached the paved drive, the front gate opened to let in the sheriff and two deputies in a car behind Landon's.

Out of the corner of his eyes he saw a couple of ranch hands with grim expressions on their faces coming toward him.

"Where's Zach?" T.J. asked Willie.

"He's out repairing the fence Cutter was

supposed to do. I'm sure he heard the shots and will be back shortly."

Two more cowhands jogged toward them while Sheriff Landon climbed from his four-wheel drive.

The law officer pushed the front of his cowboy hat up on his forehead. "We need to quit meeting like this."

"I'm in one-hundred-percent agreement, but someone else isn't." T.J. shifted toward the arriving ranch hands. "We've got everything under control, but be extra-alert. The guy who shot at Paul was driving an old red Chevy pickup, probably a late-nineties model." Then to the sheriff he added, "No license plate. But one of the dogs got hold of the man. He tore off a piece of his pants with blood on it. I'll show you."

After the sheriff had the deputies cover the back and front of the house, he went with T.J. A taut constriction around his chest still had hold of T.J. Slowly his adrenaline began to subside.

* * *

"The sheriff and a couple of deputies are here," Chloe said from her position at the side of the living room window.

"What about the dog?" Mary asked, her voice barely carrying across the space.

"The guard took him to a truck and is leaving."

"I pray he's all right," Vickie said at the entrance into the room.

So do I. "Please stay back on the stairs." Chloe gritted her teeth. "What if there's a second shooter waiting for our vigilance to drop?"

Vickie's eyes widened. "Really?"

"You have to think of as many possibilities as you can and plan for them."

Vickie backed away and retook her seat next to Aaron, who hadn't said a word since he'd run out of the house shouting for the shooter to stop. But she hadn't forgotten his words. Why would he do that unless…

She let the thought fester in the back of her

mind as she walked to the front door to unlock and open it for T.J. and the sheriff.

With grim determination stamped on his face, T.J. entered the house. "He got away in an old red Chevy pickup. Do you all know anyone who owns one like that?"

Paul rose from the step. "No, but check with Zach. He's more aware of that kind of thing."

Sheriff Landon removed his hat. "We'll keep an eye out for a vehicle like that. Without a license plate number, that's about all we can do. I'll let the police in the surrounding towns and counties know. Maybe something will turn up. In the meantime, we'll scour the area to see if we can find anything besides the torn piece of fabric."

T.J. directed his look at Aaron. "Before you leave, Sheriff, I think we need to talk with Aaron."

The teen dropped his head, his hands curling then uncurling.

In the midst of a long silence hanging over the group, Vickie hopped up. "I'm gonna see what I can fix for dinner. If you need me, I'll be in the kitchen."

"Let's go into the living room, where it's more comfortable." Chloe moved toward the entrance, then waited for the family.

Paul put his arm over Mary's shoulder, and she gave him a hug. His soft gaze glided over her face. "Next time we leave we'll need to wear soldier's helmets, too." He tipped one corner of his mouth up in a lopsided grin.

"How can you joke about what happened? You were this close to being killed." Mary indicated a couple of inches with her thumb and forefinger.

"But I'm not dead, so obviously the Lord still has things He wants me to do."

"Remember how you felt when I was bit by a rattlesnake? That's how I feel right now."

Paul sobered. "I'm sorry. I can't let this person win. He's already affected our lives. He will not affect my hope this will be taken care of soon."

When Paul, Mary and Aaron settled on the couch, T.J. stood behind the wingback chair.

"Aaron, why did you run out of the house when someone was firing at us? Why did you think you could stop him?"

Aaron lifted his chin, his mouth slashed in a frown. "He was there because of me. I paid him to play pranks to get my parents to cancel their speaking tour."

Mary gasped.

Paul grew rigid. "Why, son?"

"You canceled the skiing trip we'd planned for spring break next week because of this speaking tour. You two were gone most of the Christmas holiday. Yeah, I joined you the last part of that tour, but it isn't fun being stuck at a hotel with nothing much to do. These past two years we have seen less and less of each other and it's not because I'm at boarding school. Is that why you sent me to Bethany Academy, so you could travel more?"

"Of course not. We sent you because the school has an excellent academic program." Paul's mouth pinched together.

"We've been together this week and you've stayed in your room," Mary cried out.

"The guy didn't do what I asked. He caused a fire in Dallas. I couldn't face you all knowing that. I tried and tried to get hold of him and tell him to stop after the first two places. I left a message on his voice mail. Then at the last event you all almost got killed. Again I tried to get hold of him. I wanted to go back to Houston and find him, but she—" Aaron pointed at Chloe "—came after me."

"You should have said something. Told us." Paul's stiff posture deflated.

Aaron surged to his feet. "It got so out of hand. I don't understand. All I wanted was for the tour to be canceled. Then I thought maybe we'd go skiing together. We used to do stuff as a family all the time. I miss the ranch. I don't want to be at Bethany Academy."

"You never said anything." Tears ran down Mary's face.

"Yes, I did. You weren't listening. I mentioned finishing my last two years at the local high school. You said I would get a much better education where I was and I should finish at Bethany Academy."

T.J. came around the chair and took a seat, waving his hand at the couch. "Sit and tell us who this guy is. How did you find him? You saw firsthand his intention isn't to play pranks anymore." Out of the corner of his eye, he glimpsed the sheriff moving farther into the room, but he remained quiet.

Aaron glanced from Sheriff Landon to T.J. "One of the guys at school from Houston knew of a person who did this kind of thing. Fixed problems. I met him in a parking lot downtown. I paid him a couple hundred dollars and was to give him another couple after he finished the job. I had a phone number I was to call with any details from my parents. The letters were perfect. He delivered them to the hotel. No one saw him. The stink bombs would have been fine, but a few people were hurt. Not too bad thankfully—" the teen gulped "—but I changed my mind when I saw what could happen."

"So you told him not to do anything after Paris?" the sheriff asked from behind T.J.

"I didn't leave a message until after the first

event in Dallas when the driver of the limo was hit over the head. I thought everything was all right when nothing happened at the second speaking stop in Dallas."

"It wasn't publicized, but someone put a tracking device on the car." Chloe rose and headed for the foyer. "I have a picture I want to show you of that person we think tagged the rental. It could be your guy."

"What's his name and who is the person who told you about him?" The sheriff pulled out his pad and pen.

Fear washed over Aaron's face. He bit into his lower lip and slanted a glance toward his mother. "I'm afraid of him. Look… What he's been doing. I never told him to do that."

T.J. leaned forward, resting his elbows on his thighs. "Tell us his name. The police will catch him, and you'll be safe."

"He might be in a gang. I never asked." Aaron twisted his hands together, and his mouth clamped shut for a long moment.

His father settled his hand on the teen's shoulder. "We're here for you."

Swallowing hard, Aaron looked straight at the sheriff. "Lenny Woods—at least, that's the name I know him by."

When Chloe returned to the living room, she crossed to Aaron and showed him the picture the Dallas police had come up with from Kyra's description of the man driving the blue van.

Aaron's eyes grew wide. "That's him." He shrugged away from his dad's clasp and shoved to his feet. "This shouldn't have happened. I asked him several times to quit, and if he didn't, I wouldn't pay him any more money." His voice rose several decibels. "Are you taking me in?"

Sheriff Landon shook his head. "Not at this time. I'll be talking with the Dallas police. You'll have to answer for putting this guy into motion, but at this time, I think you're safer here under T.J. and Chloe's protection. I'll be leaving a deputy posted here until we can track down this Lenny Woods." He approached Chloe, who held the picture. "May I take that? I'll be spreading this man's sketch around and contacting Houston. Who was the student that told you about Woods?"

"Do I hafta tell you? I don't wanna get him into trouble."

"I'm afraid so, son. Your cooperation will go a long way in determining what the police in Dallas and Paris will do concerning your part in all of this."

Aaron paled, his body quaking. "Anderson Stokes."

"I'll be in touch with what we find," the sheriff said to T.J., then made his way to the front door.

Chloe followed him to let him out.

"Why didn't you say anything after your mother was bitten by the snake?" Paul asked, squeezing Mary's hand.

"I tried. I couldn't. I was—am—scared of this guy. I didn't know this would happen. Never thought it would. You're always helping every..." Aaron snapped his mouth closed.

The doorbell rang. T.J. heard Chloe answering it. Ten seconds later, Zach came into the living room with Chloe.

"Tell them what you told me." Chloe gestured to the family and T.J.

Zach took the toothpick in his mouth out and said, "Bo Moore has an old red Chevy truck. I heard from some of the cowhands about the pickup driving away from ranch. I'm sorry, Paul and Mary. Me firing him last month must have set him off."

Chloe unfolded another copy of the assailant tracking them in Dallas and showed Zach. "Is this Bo Moore?"

"Nope. There is some similarity, but Bo has a cleft in his chin. This guy doesn't and his eyes are blue, not brown. Hair is lighter, almost blond. I told the sheriff before he left and he's going to get a warrant for Moore's house and see if he can find his truck."

"There are two people?" Paul's eyebrows scrunched together.

"I didn't hire two people." Aaron collapsed on the couch and laid his head on the back cushion, closing his eyes. "This is a nightmare. How did it get so out of control?"

"Okay." T.J. held up his hand. "It won't do us any good to start speculating about what has happened. Thanks for the information, Zach. Hopefully the sheriff and police here or in Houston will find the truck and Bo Moore as well as this Lenny Woods. At least now we have some names to follow up on."

While Chloe walked with Zach to the door, Mary looked up at T.J. "We would like some private time with our son. Is it okay in here?"

"Yes. I'll make sure no one bothers you." T.J. strode to all the windows in the living room and closed the blinds. "I'll be doing that in the whole house."

T.J. met Chloe in the foyer. "Let's shut the blinds. We might as well not give a sniper a target."

"I just got off the phone with Kyra. She said one of the references for Dave Cutter checked out. The other two didn't."

"Which means?" T.J. stood at the bottom of the staircase.

"He's worked at one ranch for about six months. No other experience. Zach told me he called the first one and the man had good things to say about Dave. Zach had been short a cowhand for a while and with spring approaching he decided to hire him on a trial basis. At that time, nothing had happened in Dallas and Zach thought the Paris incident was just a disgruntled person."

"I'll take care of the windows downstairs while you do the upstairs."

T.J. met Chloe back in the foyer five minutes later.

"Aaron's bedroom is a mess. That's unusual. Mary told me he's neater than she is."

He shook his head. "I knew on the trip to the San Antonio hospital that something was wrong with Aaron. I should have pressured him to talk."

"He wasn't ready. He's in trouble now and will have to face the consequences. It could be jail time, depending on what the police and DA discover." Chloe snapped her fingers. "I almost forgot. The other guard got a call. The German shepherd will be okay. The second guard will get another dog and return soon. I suggest we keep two patrolling outside and also that wooded area across the ranch road."

"Agreed. I'll make the arrangement with the agency to double up. I'm hoping Lenny will be found soon and this will all end."

"Maybe for us, but not for Mary, Aaron and Paul."

T.J. started to step toward her but stopped himself. It shouldn't be long before this assignment was over. Until then he needed to rein in his feelings for Chloe. Afterward, he had decisions to make. He was falling for her again, but then, he had nine years ago and neither of them had been able to make the commitment to the other. He didn't want to go through that again.

"I thought you were taking a nap," Chloe said when she entered the kitchen and found Mary staring into her mug in front of her on the table.

"I can't. I don't think I got two hours' sleep last night. I keep waiting—praying for the phone to ring and the sheriff to tell us the person who's been doing this has been caught."

Chloe eased into the chair across from Mary. "It's only been twenty-four hours. No one knows where Bo Moore or his truck is. The sheriff talked with Bo's brother in Phoenix, and he wasn't due to show up for the new job for another week, so Bo told his brother he would hang around here a few more days with some of his friends."

"Did the sheriff talk with his friends?"

"Yes and they haven't seen him in over a day. He'd mentioned to one of them he had an opportunity to make a little cash before he left for Arizona."

Mary's eyes widened.

"Don't worry. The sheriff has everyone looking for him and his pickup. It's been on the news in this county and the surrounding ones."

"I hope something gives soon. Look at me." Mary held her trembling hand out flat. "I've prayed and prayed. Paul has and even Aaron joined us last night." She made a fist that shook, too. "Then we have to deal with what our son has done."

"Did you call your lawyer this morning?"

"Yes, and he'll be here this evening to talk to Aaron and us." She laughed, but there was no humor in the sound. "We go around the country talking about taking back our communities and not tolerating violence. How can we do that with what Aaron set in motion? What kind of authority are we now?"

"I never got the feeling from your message you were speaking from a place of authority. More from a place of concern for the type of future we'll leave our children. You're a parent. You have a right to talk about that. I hope more will start being concerned about where our future is going and take a stand."

Tears in her eyes, Mary swallowed over and over. "I've cried so much in the past week. In the middle of this, about all I can really do is turn it over to the Lord. I can't function on two hours of sleep a night. I've got to find a way to push this worry away and keep my eye on God. This has been my biggest test. I tell people to do that, and now I'm struggling to keep my focus on the Lord myself."

"Because it isn't easy. It can be one of the most difficult things a person does in the midst of a crisis. Let the worry go. I've done my fair share of worrying over the years, and I'm sure I will in the future. We want to control everything, and we worry when we can't."

"Thanks." Mary tried to smile while a wet tear coursed down her face. "I need to listen to the advice I've given others." She swiped her hand across her cheeks. "I'm not the type of person to have a pity party. Let's talk about something other than my situation." This time one corner of her mouth lifted. "What's going on between you and T.J.?"

Had Aaron said something to his mother about the kiss she and T.J. shared last night? "What do you mean?" she finally said while trying to decide how to handle this conversation.

"I've seen how you look at T.J. Not often,

but every once in a while. I may have missed the signals my son was sending me, but I think you care about T.J.—more than just as a partner. Am I right?"

Chloe stared into Mary's understanding eyes and knew she could trust the woman with her emotions, which seesawed between committing herself to T.J. and seeing if they could work out as a couple and cutting her losses and making a change in her life that she'd been thinking about for months.

"Yes, but it's complicated."

"Love often is."

Love? She wanted to deny that, but the words wouldn't come out. "I grew up in a family with a father who was rarely around. I saw what it did to my mother. He broke her heart. I vowed that I would come first in a man's life—first before a job—but then I fell in love with T.J. nine years ago. I knew I shouldn't and I was right. He got a promotion and moved to Washington, D.C."

"He just picked up and left without talking to you about it?"

"Well, no. He wanted me to follow him after my mother was better. For me to leave my job and my mother, who had just recovered from cancer, I couldn't. What if it hadn't worked out? What if..."

Mary covered Chloe's hand on the table. "We can't predict the future. All we can do is believe in the Lord and trust Him to lead us in the right direction. If you aren't ready to commit to T.J. one hundred percent, then you shouldn't. But don't try second-guessing what might happen in the future. I never in my wildest dream thought what my family is going through would happen. And I'm glad I didn't know ahead of time. I would have spent all that time worrying. Worrying doesn't change the situation and often compounds it. When you became an adult, what did you see your future as?"

"I wanted to be a wife and mother."

"In spite of what happened to your parents?"

"I love children. It was a dream I had since I was a young teenager. It wasn't until I was seventeen that I really saw what was going on with my mother and father. She'd tried to shield me from her problems, but when my father took back-to-back assignments so he would be gone much longer from home, she fell apart. From then on, I was who she confided in."

"That's quite a burden for a teenager."

"She needed me. I had to be there for her."

"Yes, but you are not your mother and your situation isn't the same."

Uncertain about what to think anymore, Chloe rose. "I'm not so sure."

"Pray, Chloe. Talk to the Lord."

Chloe started to say something, but the sound of someone approaching the room filtered through her confusion. She swallowed back the words.

T.J. walked into the kitchen, holding his cell phone to his ear. "Thanks for letting us know. I'll pass the information on to Paul and Mary."

When he hung up and looked at them, Chloe knew the news wasn't good. Although his expression showed little emotion, the taut lines of his body conveyed a different impression.

"That was Sheriff Landon. They found Bo Moore in his pickup in a lake. A rifle was in the cab with him."

THIRTEEN

"Is it over?" Mary massaged her temples.

"No. Moore may be responsible for the shooting earlier, but we have no reason behind the attack. Lenny Woods is still out there." T.J. slipped his cell phone into his pocket. "I'm going to let Paul know. At least we probably won't have someone out there shooting at us, and the sheriff said the Houston police have a lead on where Lenny is— the hospital. Apparently he got into a fight two days ago and ended up shot."

"Will he recover?" Chloe rolled her knotted shoulders, then kneaded her fingers into her nape. At least some answers were falling into place.

"The sheriff didn't have all the details, but he's coming by later to talk with Aaron. I told him your lawyer would arrive at six, so he'll be here then. Maybe he'll have more information for us at that time."

"How did he end up in a lake?" Something bothered Chloe about that, but she didn't know what.

"From what little the sheriff could figure out, Moore lost control of his truck."

"Were there any witnesses?" Chloe crossed to the pot of coffee on the stove and poured a mugful.

"No. A passerby from the road saw the rear end barely sticking out of the water early this morning."

Mary took her teacup to the sink. "All this discussion has tired me out. I'm going to see if I can sleep some before the lawyer and sheriff come. Vickie thought she would prepare some sandwiches and buffet-type food, so if Sheriff Landon and Henry Calvin want to have something to eat, they can. No telling how long all of this will take tonight." Hugging her arms to her, she shivered. "But this meeting will have far-reaching consequences for Aaron and for all of us."

When Mary had disappeared down the hall, T.J. grabbed a cup of coffee, too. "She looks exhausted."

"She's not sleeping."

"Paul isn't, either."

"Where is he?"

"With Aaron, in his office. Aaron is writing down everything he remembers surrounding hiring Lenny to cause trouble on the speaking tour."

"Where did Aaron get that kind of cash?"

"He worked last summer and had it in his saving account. He's finally telling his dad how unhappy he's been at Bethany Academy. I decided to leave them alone. I think Aaron will talk more freely without me in the office."

"A breakdown in communication can destroy a relationship. I'm glad to see them finally talking."

"Like you and me?"

Chloe tilted her head and studied him a

moment. "Yes. We should have talked more in the past. I think, though, we were in two different places in our lives." And she was beginning to feel they were in two different places now. Talking to Mary over the course of this assignment, as well as just a few minutes ago, Chloe realized she wanted more from life than what she had. She wanted roots and a family. She didn't want a husband wrapped up in his job. Look at what was happening to the Zimmermans because their work took over their lives. "Some people are meant only to be friends."

His look sliced through her. "Us?"

"You're looking at going into business with Kyra and expanding it. That's going to require a lot of time and work. I'm looking at simplifying my life. I've realized I haven't read a good book in years because I'm always working. I have an apartment in Dallas, but no pets because I'm always gone. In fact, my place doesn't feel like a home. It means no more to me than a hotel room. I've been thinking about what Mary and Paul say about considering what's really important in life. Is it money? Is it possessions? What rules your life? At the moment, my job rules mine and I'm finding out that's not what I want. I want more." Chloe started for the back door. "I'm going to walk around the house. I need some fresh air, and I want to make sure everyone is doing what they need to."

T.J. called out to her as she left, but she kept going. She needed a change. She wasn't sure what she would do, but she needed something different.

Chloe opened the front door to let the Zimmermans' attorney, Mr. Calvin, into the house that evening. She noticed that the sheriff was pulling up. "The family is in the living room. Go on in. Sheriff Landon has arrived. I'll wait for him."

Passing the lawyer in the entrance into the room, T.J. approached her with a determined expression on his face. She'd been avoiding him the whole afternoon. For the past half a year, she'd been dissatisfied with what she was doing. She'd always love helping people feel safe, but not this way. She'd dodged one too many bullets.

Instead of staying inside, she moved out onto the verandah as the sheriff headed toward the house. The smile on the man's face prompted her to ask, "Do you have good news?"

"Yep." The sheriff's gaze shifted to a place behind her. "The Houston police found Lenny Woods getting ready to leave the hospital. They took him down to the station and are questioning him now. The detective will call me with any additional information after the interrogation. They searched his place and found a few hundred dollars, which fits what Aaron said. Also they found a burner phone with half a dozen messages on it from the teen. The last one was a plea to stop what he was doing before he killed someone."

Chloe stepped to the side, spying T.J. behind her. "Come in. They're in the living room. Your news isn't going to get Aaron off the hook, but it will help his case."

Her gaze latched on to T.J.'s as he entered the house. She started across the foyer.

T.J. blocked her. "We need to talk."

"About what? Leaving the ranch?"

"No. About us. You're doing exactly what you did nine years ago. I think we have a chance as a couple, but I sense you're backing away from me. What do you want from me? I've moved to Dallas. I'm going to be doing what you're doing."

"Is this why you came to Dallas? To see if you and I could make a second go of it?"

Fury hardened his features. "Yes. I didn't realize it, but it was the reason I came here. I could have moved anywhere and made a fresh start. I chose here because we did have something special once—enough that you spoiled me for any other woman."

Her eyes blinked wide. "I did? Don't blame that on me." She pushed past him and marched across the foyer to plant herself in the entrance into the living room. She clenched her hands so hard pain spread up her arms. This wasn't the time to make that important decision she'd talked with Mary about earlier.

T.J. joined her, leaning close to her ear. "You're scared. You think I'll be like your father—an absentee husband. I'm not your father. If I make a commitment, I put my whole self into it."

She turned her head slightly. "As you did your job all these years?" Before he could reply, she put her finger to her lips and said, "Shh." She couldn't deal with this now.

T.J. lounged against the opposite doorjamb with a look of thunder on his face.

With T.J. feet from her, Chloe had a hard time focusing on the interview between the sheriff and Aaron. Sheriff Landon finished walking the teen through what he'd done to procure Lenny Woods's services and why. Paul sat on one side of his son while Mary was on the other. She could imagine what was going through their minds as they listened again to their son explain he'd needed more from his parents and had gone about getting it the wrong way. So much of what

Aaron said reminded Chloe of how she'd felt as a teenager, especially toward her father.

At the end of the interview Sheriff Landon said, "After I was notified about Lenny Woods being taken into custody in Houston, I called Detective Matthews. Tomorrow he's driving to Houston to interrogate Woods and arrange for the man to be transported to Dallas. He wanted to know if I felt y'all were out of danger. I told him yes. We had a few loose ends to tie up, but it appeared the two perpetrators involved have been accounted for."

"Did you ever find Dave Cutter?" Chloe asked, wondering where the man had gone.

"He left because his divorced wife was closing in on him for child support. He's disappeared again." The sheriff shook his head. "That's a pity for his children."

The lawyer sat forward. "What about Aaron?"

"Detective Matthews wants Aaron to turn himself in the day after tomorrow before noon in Dallas. That'll give you time to drive there from the ranch. Okay?"

Mr. Calvin glanced at Paul before answering, "Yes. I'll be accompanying the Zimmermans to the police station in Dallas. Aaron wants to cooperate with the police any way he can."

The sheriff stood and shook the lawyer's hand and then Paul's. "I'm sorry all this happened, but at least now you can go about your life without worrying about someone being after you."

"But we don't know why Bo Moore did it," Paul said.

"My guess, since he can't tell us, is that he was madder than Zach had thought about being fired from the ranch, and since you're the owner, he saw you as the one behind the smoking ban. The rifle he had in the cab of his pickup was like the one used by the sniper in the pecan grove. The ballistics checked out. They matched." Sheriff Landon plopped his hat on his head and made his way toward the foyer.

T.J. walked with the man to the front door.

Chloe stayed, not wanting to be alone with T.J. at the moment.

"What's going to happen to me?" Aaron began pacing in front of the fireplace.

"I'm going to try to have this taken care of in juvenile court since you're still sixteen." The lawyer stood, buttoning his suit coat.

"Will me being seventeen in a couple of months make a difference?"

"Maybe, but we should be able to show your intent and what you did to change what was happening. That might help your case. But I'm not going to kid you. You could serve time and your parents may be open to lawsuits. We need to expect the worst and hope for something better, which is probation and community service."

"You will have to face the consequences, but you won't be alone. We'll be by your side." Paul bridged the distance between him and his son and embraced him. "You should have come forward sooner, but at least you did."

"I've ruined everything for you and Mom."

"The Lord wants us to go down this path for a reason. He's never wrong. Maybe He has other plans for your mom and me. We'll just have to wait and see."

Mr. Calvin gathered up his papers and stuffed them in his briefcase, then rose. "I'll be talking with the prosecutor in Dallas tomorrow. I'll let you know what he says."

"Thank you, Henry. I'll walk you out. It will be nice to be able to go outside without worrying about someone being after us." Paul accompanied the lawyer to the door.

"This meeting didn't take as long as we thought. I forgot to invite the sheriff and Henry to dinner." Mary stood, closing her eyes for a few seconds, weariness in every line of her body. "I hate for Vickie's buffet to go to waste, but I'm too tired to eat. I'm going to bed early."

"Mom?"

She smiled at Aaron. "I'm fine, honey. Y'all have to remember I was in the hospital recently and don't have the energy I usually have." Mary strolled toward her. "Chloe, maybe you can see if any of the ranch hands are still here. If so, they're invited to dinner. Since Zach lives on the ranch, at least he should come."

"I'll walk down to the barn and check with Zach. We'll take care of the food. Won't we, Aaron?"

"Don't worry. I'm starved. I'll eat your share."

"Thanks. At least tonight I should be able to sleep. And, Aaron, I'm not worrying. Not when I remember who is really in charge."

Chloe watched Mary climb the stairs slowly. Sleep was the best thing for her right now. "Aaron, your mom is a strong woman. She'll be fine."

"I know." The teen paused next to Chloe. "I'd like to come with you to the barn. Okay?"

Chloe glimpsed T.J. and Paul entering the house. "Sure. Let's go out the back." She didn't want to talk to T.J. She had some serious praying and thinking to do. She didn't want to mess up her future and act recklessly.

Besides a change, what do I want?

* * *

Chloe descended the stairs to the foyer and set her piece of luggage by the door. After breakfast, she and T.J. would leave the ranch. Although they had offered to stay an extra day and follow them back to Dallas, Mary and Paul had insisted they were fine and needed some alone time with their son before he turned himself into the police. They needed to feel their life was normal at least for a day.

T.J. called Sheriff Landon and he said the Houston authorities were interrogating Lenny Woods. "He hadn't said much except he wanted a lawyer. But Lenny couldn't give an alibi for the event at the theater in Dallas. He said he had been sleeping off a hangover in a Dallas motel at the time. I called the place he said he was staying, and the manager couldn't say one way or another if he had been there the afternoon in question."

When she entered the kitchen, Mary, Paul and Aaron were already seated as Vickie set a platter of blueberry pancakes in the middle of the table, and then took a chair.

T.J. finished pouring a cup of coffee and held up the pot. "Want some?"

"Yes." Chloe sat at one of the two places left, realizing T.J. would be next to her. Last night she should have gotten a good night's sleep, but for hours she'd kept replaying scenes from when she and T.J. had dated years ago. She'd gotten out of bed and paced her bedroom, thinking about their time together, especially at the ranch. The kisses they had shared had flashed in and out of her thoughts until she'd given up trying to get any rest. She'd lain down and stared at the ceiling in the darkness, and some time in the night she'd finally fallen asleep in exhaustion, a prayer for help running through her mind. She'd barely dragged herself out of bed half an hour ago.

T.J. took the seat next to her and slid her mug toward her. She reached for it, needing the caffeine.

"What are all of you planning to do today?" Chloe asked after several sips of her coffee.

"I need to go shopping later." Vickie poured hot maple syrup over her pancakes. "I'm thankful one of the ranch hands did it for us, but it's hard to think of everything we need and put it down on a list. I've never been a person who could only shop by what I had on a list."

"I appreciate you taking over the household account while I've been gone so much, but Paul and I have decided we aren't leaving for the next year. All this has made us reconsider what we need and want to do." Mary patted Aaron's hand. "I want my son to feel he's the most important one in our lives."

"We're thinking of riding over the ranch after lunch. Getting out and enjoying this beautiful day God created and reconnect with Him. We haven't done that in nine months. Then we'll prepare ourselves for what's to come concerning Aaron." Paul snatched another piece of bacon off a plate in the center of the table. "How about you and T.J.?"

"I don't know about T.J., but I'm crashing for a few days. I forgot to water my one plant, a cactus, and I'm afraid it might have bit the dust by now. I used to have more houseplants, but traveling makes it hard to keep any."

"I have Vickie. She takes care of us." Mary smiled at her cousin across from her.

"So what are you going to do next, T.J.?" Paul stabbed his fork into pieces of pancake.

T.J. glanced sideways at Chloe. "I'll be finalizing my partnership with Kyra Hunt. She called this morning to tell me she has accepted my offer."

"Congratulations. That's great. You and Chloe are good at your job. We appreciate you two." Paul took a bite of his pancake. "But we're ecstatic we don't need you all anymore."

Chloe had been pretty sure Kyra would take T.J. on as a partner, but with her second pregnancy, how much would she be involved in the business? Would he be out in the field any or working at the main office? How much did he want to expand? T.J. knew the business and could go far, especially with his background and connections. He wanted to go forward. She wanted to go in a different direction. Again they were at divergent places in their lives.

When breakfast was over, Mary hugged Chloe, whispering, "I recently discovered what's more important in my life than my work. My family. I hope you get your heart's desire and find those answers you're searching for." Mary looked at T.J., then pointedly back to Chloe. "You saved my life. I imagine you have done that for others, too. That's a gift the Lord gave you. I wish you the best, and don't be a stranger. I want to stay in touch."

After saying their goodbyes, Chloe and T.J. climbed into his Jeep for the three-hour drive to Dallas. Chloe had a lot to think about, especially Mary's parting words. For the first few minutes as they left the ranch behind, a strained silence dominated the atmosphere in the car.

Then T.J. said, "What I didn't say back in

the kitchen was that Kyra won't be coming back to the agency. I'll slowly buy her out and have full ownership, probably in the next two years. How do you feel about that?" Tension wove through his words, his hands clenching the steering wheel.

She told him what Mary had said to her at the end, and then added, "I don't know."

"Why not? When I first saw you and talked with you, I never felt you were unhappy with your job. Did this assignment, working with me, make you unhappy?"

She chewed her lower lip, trying to figure out what to say. "I'm not unhappy about my work, just not satisfied like I used to be. The more I was around you, the more I began to think about what I used to dream about and what I have put on the back burner for all these years. A family. I need more than my job. I need to feel grounded and I'm not right now."

"Are you telling me you're leaving Guardians, Inc.?"

"I don't want to continue as I have, on the

road three-fourths of the time. What husband would want his wife traveling all the time?" She immediately thought of Adam and her father. "I know what that does to a relationship."

T.J. pulled off the road and parked the Jeep, then twisted toward her. "I love you, Chloe. I think we can make it work. I want a family, too. I don't want to pass this second chance up for us. I told you when I make a commitment I make a total one. If I stand before God and pledge myself to you, you will have me one hundred percent."

"I don't see how you can do that with the plans you have for Guardians, Inc. I don't want a husband that is married to his job, too. I need more. I see that now. You're right. That was why in the end I didn't come to Washington after my mother's chemo treatments were finished. I used that as an excuse. It was hard enough for us to find time together with me being a cop and you a Secret Service agent working in the counterfeiting unit."

He reached for her hand and held it. "Let

me make myself clear. I'll run the agency, not be a bodyguard. I've gotten a lot out of my work, but it's time for me to move on to something a little different. I want you to be my partner in marriage and in the business. I'm looking to expand, which means more work running the agency. I can't think of a better person to work with because I wouldn't want you traveling for your job. I want to go home to you every night. I want to be there for you and you for me. I want to stay in one place and make a home filled with love and the Lord."

She tugged her hand from his grasp. His touch made her forget her rational side, and this was too important to let feelings swamp her, with no regard to the consequences of her decision. This was for the rest of her life. "I want children. At least two. I used to baby-sit as a teenager and loved being with kids. I even considered becoming a teacher, but police work called to me more."

"I'd love to be the father of your children. You can work as much as you want at the agency. As I said, we will be equal partners in all things. This assignment showed me how well we work together. I think the Lord brought us back together again because we're perfect for each other."

The emotions she tried to hold at bay overwhelmed her. There had never been another man for her, but would this really work? Could they make the change they needed? *Is this Your answer to my prayers, Lord?* "Are you sure once you get back and take over the agency you won't get sucked into your job? Look at what the Zimmermans' career did to their family."

"If we have good employees in place, we don't have to work all the time. Kyra has made it work. It can be a regular job. So what do you say about going into partnership with me? And to make myself clear, I mean in marriage *and* the agency."

"I love you, T.J. I always have, but I need some time to think. I'm exhausted from this job, and I don't want to rush into a lifelong commitment without making sure it's what is best for the both of us. You need to do the same thing. It'll be a big change for us. We've been on our own for years."

He cocked a grin. "Always the practical one. Okay." He took her hand and pulled her toward him. Framing her face, he touched his forehead to hers. "If we get married, I'm more afraid I'm not going to want to even go to work. You'll have to kick me out of the house or we might starve."

He kissed her, laying claim to her with heart-shattering possession. When he straightened and switched on the engine, he threw her a look that melted any reservation she had. In that moment she knew it was the Lord's answer to her prayers last night. She loved him. He loved her. She needed to put her faith in that and cherish the time they had together rather than be governed by her past.

"T.J.—"

His cell phone rang, spoiling the moment.

"That's Sheriff Landon." He answered it. His smile quickly evolved into a frown. "Thanks for the information. We're going to turn around and head back to the ranch. We're about ten minutes away. I'll call you later."

"What's wrong?"

T.J. made a U-turn. "Sheriff Landon got the autopsy report back on Bo Moore. He was full of sleeping pills and tranquilizers. He drowned, but he was unconscious when it happened. They're going to scour where the truck went off the road. He doesn't think it's a suicide, especially when he talked with Bo's girlfriend. Yes, he was angry about losing his job, but he was mad at Zach. Bo and his girl-friend were planning to elope next weekend and settle in Arizona. Doesn't sound like a suicidal man."

"No. So that means we don't know who shot at the Zimmermans when they returned from the celebration at the church."

"It's possible they still aren't safe. He called the Houston police, and Lenny Woods keeps saying the last thing he did before he received Aaron's message was put a tracking device on the rental car and follow us from the second event in Dallas."

"Which leaves the fire at the theater, the snakes and the sniper. Do you think someone took advantage of the fact someone was after the Zimmermans?"

"Yes." T.J. increased his speed. "I can't see Nancy doing it, because she's no longer the publicist for the Zimmermans. She has nothing to gain going after them. I'm the one who got her fired, so if she is angry, it should be at me." He tossed her glance. "But we can't rule out anyone."

"Someone at the ranch or in town? Or we could be back to someone upset at the Zimmermans' message. They're particularly vocal about gangs in communities."

"When we get back to the ranch, we'll sit down with them and go through the people they know again."

At the gate he phoned the main house, but no one answered. Then T.J. placed a call to Zach, who had the ability to let someone into the ranch from his office. T.J. knew yesterday's gate code, but he'd trained Paul to change it every morning.

As they approached the main house, Chloe pushed her exhaustion away and focused on the job to be done if someone was still after the Zimmermans. The second the Jeep stopped, she was out of it and striding toward the front door. She rang the bell while T.J. joined her on the verandah. When no one came to answer, she pressed the button again and rested her hand on her gun.

The door swung open, and Vickie appeared in the entrance. "Sorry. I was in the kitchen making a list of items I needed at the store. Did you forget something?"

"No, but I don't think this is over yet. Where are Paul and Mary?" T.J. looked beyond Vickie into the foyer.

Vickie glanced over her shoulder. "They went to meet the lawyer in town. Some new development concerning the charges against Aaron. He went with them. I was finishing up and gathering my purse, so I can go meet them there for lunch before I go shopping." Hugging her handbag under her arm, she rambled.

T.J. barged past her. "We'll follow you, but first I want to search the house to make sure everything is okay since security hasn't been tight the past eighteen hours. Someone could have snuck something in here. You all stay there. I won't be too long."

While he went into the living room, Chloe skirted Vickie to stand inside the entrance. T.J. came back out and headed across the foyer to the dining room.

"Vickie, where are you? I'm here to finish the job," a deep masculine voice said from the kitchen.

Mary's cousin's eyes grew round. She took a step back, then whirled and raced out the front door.

Near the dining room door into the kitchen, T.J. smelled gas. Coming from the kitchen? They had a gas stove. Something wasn't right.

Then he heard Shane call out to Vickie. He slapped his palm against the swinging door and pushed his way into the kitchen. He caught sight of Mary and Paul lying on the floor.

His attention was riveted on Shane, who was standing near them, surprise registering on his craggy face. He turned and ran for the back door. T.J. flew across the room and threw himself at the ranch hand. They fell to the floor, T.J.'s arms locked around the man's chest. Shane flung T.J.'s body back against a set of cabinets nearby. Then he did again. T.J.'s head struck the wooden door. His ears ringing, he hung on and tightened his hold.

Shane grunted and tried to shake T.J. off him. Bringing his hands up, Shane clutched T.J.'s arms and pulled down. He broke T.J.'s grip on him. The ranch hand rotated at the same time, scrambling back from T.J. Shane brought his fist back and drilled it into T.J. Through the haze in his head, T.J. returned a punch. Then another. The stench of gas filled his nostrils, and he knew he needed to get the family out of there. Soon.

* * *

Vickie was halfway down the sidewalk, not far from her car, which was parked in front of T.J.'s.

Chloe drew her Glock and aimed it at the woman. "Halt or I'll shoot."

Vickie glanced back and veered onto the grass but tripped over a stone. She went down on her knees, and Chloe fired her weapon off to the side of the woman to scare her.

Vickie froze, lifting her shaking arms. "Okay. Okay."

"Lie face down on the grass and don't move. All I can think about is that I hate snakes, and you're probably the one who put two in your cousin's greenhouse." Chloe approached her, keeping her attention focused on Vickie.

The sound of pounding footsteps forced Chloe to look briefly toward the barn. Zach. Still not sure who to trust at the ranch, she shouted, "Go get some rope to tie her up." Then she watched to see if he would.

Chloe let out a bottled breath when the foreman headed back to the barn. She knew that T.J. could take care of himself, but who was the man who had shouted from the kitchen?

A shot rang through the air, fueling T.J.'s determination to finish this, to get the family outside and check on Chloe. He willed all his strength behind his next blow to Shane's jaw. Pain streaked up his arm as his fist connected with the man's face. But the hit flattened Shane back on the floor, his head cracking against the tiles. Shane passed out, his body going limp.

T.J. didn't waste any time. He scrambled to his feet, clutching the side of the counter to get his bearings then he hurried and switched off the stove and closed the oven. Mary lay nearby, and he picked her up. After carrying her outside, he checked to make sure Shane was still out and dragged Paul out the back door. In the corner, he spied Aaron slumped against the wall. T.J. had little strength left but managed to haul the teen to the doorway. Stepping outside, he sucked in a deep breath of fresh air, then continued with Aaron out the back and down the steps to the back-yard—away from the house.

When he returned to the kitchen, he used the cords on the blinds to tie Shane up, then pulled the man free of the house. As he headed to the front, he called the sheriff, explained briefly what had happened and requested some ambulances.

With gun in hand, he rounded the corner to the front yard to find Zach tying up Vickie while Chloe held her Glock on the woman. When Vickie was secured, Chloe's shoulders sagged slightly, but she still kept her gun at her side as though prepared for anything else.

As he approached, she peered at him and grinned.

"I'm glad you caught Vickie. I took Shane down in the kitchen. The gas was on. I turned it off and got everyone outside. The family was passed out on the floor."

Zach straightened, glaring at Vickie as he dragged her to her feet. "Why did you do this? Mary and Paul gave you everything."

"And they never let me forget that they took me in and saved me from bankruptcy. All my life Mary got everything. Paul. An important job. A big house and ranch. People who loved her. I always got her leftovers. When I was a child living with her family. When I was adult and had financial problems. I was tired of always coming in second and having to be nice or fear I'd be kicked out of the house."

Zach shook his head. "Mary and Paul aren't like that, but you're too full of hate to see the goodness in them."

"Look what they did to their own son. Shuffled him off to boarding school. They couldn't be bothered to raise him and when he was home, I had to play mother because Mary was too busy." Venom dripped from each word.

"Keep an eye on her, Zach. I'm going to the backyard to check on Paul, Mary and Aaron." T.J. grabbed Chloe's hand and tugged her to his side.

As they walked around the house, he slung his arm around Chloe. "When I heard a gun go off, I was so afraid you'd been hurt. It gave me the extra incentive to finish off Shane."

"Shane was helping Vickie?"

"I knocked him out, but when he wakes up, we'll see what his story is. Vickie had to have outside help. She may have put the snakes in the greenhouse, but Shane had to be the one who fired at us after the celebration. You know it was Shane that pointed us toward Bo Moore and his red pickup."

"I thought Vickie was interested in Shane. Obviously more than I thought."

T.J. rounded the corner and immediately found the couple and their son where he'd left them. Paul was leaning over Mary while Aaron stirred on the ground nearby.

T.J. hurried to their side with Chloe next to him. "Are you okay?"

Confusion clouding his eyes, Paul glanced up. "She's alive, but still out. What happened to us?"

"An ambulance and the sheriff are coming. Vickie had the gas on. I found you three passed out on the floor. Do you remember anything?"

"Mary and Vickie were in the kitchen talking at the table. I came in to talk with Vickie about some discrepancies I found in the account books." He looked to Aaron, who sat up, touching the back of his head and wincing. "What's wrong, son?"

Aaron brought his hand around and showed them his bloodied fingers. "She...hit me."

"Vickie?" Chloe asked.

"Yes." Aaron closed his eyes for a few seconds. "I came into the kitchen—saw my parents on the floor." He peered at his mom. "Mom." He started to get up, but collapsed back onto the ground.

Chloe went to Aaron and knelt next to him. "She'll be all right." She glimpsed Mary moving her hand. "See. You need to stay put until the paramedics get here."

The blare of the siren echoed through the air.

Before the couple and Aaron were taken

away, T.J. squatted next to Paul. "Why were you looking at the books this morning?"

"Zach told me there was something wrong. I thought I would see before we had to leave for Dallas. When I said that to Vickie, she smiled and agreed we should do it now. With what was happening, I thought she had probably added a few things wrong. She went to the coffeepot and poured a cup for me and refilled Mary's, then sat to talk about the accounts."

Mary moaned. "The last thing I remember…" Her voice sputtered to a halt. She blinked. "…is you opening the books on the table."

"Yeah, you fell over as I was talking with Vickie."

"Did you drink some coffee?" T.J. noticed the paramedics coming around the side of the house, relieved help had arrived.

"Yes. You think she drugged us?"

"Probably. Was she drinking the coffee?" T.J. caught sight of Sheriff Landon right behind the EMTs.

Paul frowned. "No, and she loves coffee." He snorted. "I didn't get very far going through the books with her before I must have blacked out."

"I guess she was going to use the gas leak to cover everything up. When it builds up, it doesn't take much for an explosion." T.J. stood and backed away as paramedics started working on the family and readying them for transportation.

After making sure the Zimmermans would be all right, Sheriff Landon crossed to where Shane lay, trying to get free. The sheriff slapped his handcuffs on the cowhand. "You aren't going anywhere. I'm taking you to the station along with Vickie. We have all day to straighten this out." He hauled Shane to his feet, then looked toward T.J. and Chloe a few feet away. "I guess you two will have to stay around another day. When Mary, Paul and Aaron are taken care of, I'd like to see you two at the station, too. I intend to close this case once and for all."

"That you'll be able to do. We'll be there

shortly. Tell your men to be careful in the house. Vickie had the gas on in the kitchen." T.J. slipped his arm around Chloe.

The sheriff tipped his hat, then strode with Shane toward the front.

"If you hadn't pulled over to talk to me about our future, we might not have made it back in time to save them." Chloe nestled closer to T.J, turning her head up toward his and reaching up to kiss him on the lips. "Yes."

T.J.'s gaze gleamed with love. "Yes? To what?"

"Yes, I'll marry you. In the car before the sheriff called you, I was going to tell you I didn't need time to think it over. But then the timing wasn't right and possibly the timing isn't right now, but I don't want to risk any more time passing without telling you."

He bent his head toward her and returned her kiss. "I love you."

"Good because I love you, too. I don't want to take a chance and lose you. Life's too short, and if we love each other, we can work anything out. And I do love you. I've never stopped loving you. No man lived up to you in my eyes."

T.J. embraced her and swung her around. "It might have taken us a while to figure out we're perfect for each other, but I'm not going to let you forget one day of our marriage how important you are to me." He'd finally found a place to call home—anywhere with Chloe.

EPILOGUE

Ten months later

"Is my husband busy?" Chloe asked T.J.'s secretary when she came into the office.

"No, he just got off the phone."

Chloe crossed to his door and went into the room to find T.J. working at his desk. He looked up, and his dark eyes gleamed. A slow smile spread across his face as he rose.

"What did the doctor say?" T.J. covered the distance to her and drew her into his arms.

"It's official. I'm pregnant. In seven months you will be a daddy."

He beamed. "That's the best news you could tell me."

She stretched up on her tiptoes and gave

him a quick kiss on his mouth. "We need to celebrate tonight."

"A few minutes ago Paul called to tell me the verdict in Vickie's trial came in. Guilty of murder and attempted murder as well as the arson at the theater. Paul saw Rob at the trial. He was still upset that he carried the woman out of the fire who was responsible for setting it."

"Vickie was wearing a good disguise. She was a bitter, sad woman. For years, her envy of Mary festered, and when the pranks started, she hatched this plot to finally get rid of Mary. She didn't care if she took Paul and Aaron with her. She was set from embezzling money out of the Zimmermans' accounts."

"I felt sorry for Shane. He loved her, and she used him. She'd planned to leave the country with the money she'd stolen, leaving him behind. She didn't think he would say anything because he was involved, too. Actually, Vickie and Shane killed Bo Moore to set him up to be their patsy."

"With Lenny's, then Shane's trial a cou-

ple of months ago, that's the last person involved in Paul and Mary's harassment and
attempted murder. It's over." Chloe inhaled a
deep breath, the scent of lime aftershave filling her nostrils. She would always associate
that smell with T.J.

"Paul wanted to take us to dinner before
he and Mary drive back to the ranch. I said
yes. Okay?"

The warmth of his look made her feel cherished. "Sure. We can celebrate when we get
home. I want to share the news with them. If
it hadn't been for Mary and Paul, we might
not be married today."

He cuddled closer. "Oh, I don't know about
that. After all, I came back to Dallas because
of you."

"And it took you six months to figure that
out. Is Aaron with them?" She would never
tire of being in T.J.'s embrace.

"No. He's finishing up his community service at home. He can't miss any school unless
he's sick. He's staying with his pastor's family
until Paul and Mary return home tomorrow."

"Then all he has is four more years on probation until he turns twenty-one."

"According to Paul, Aaron has changed. He's involved with learning how to run the ranch. Paul is, too."

"It took a tragedy to make them a family again."

T.J. bent his head and settled his lips over hers. "A lesson we need to remember. Not to let our work consume us."

"Nothing is more important than you and this baby."

* * * * *

Dear Reader,

Welcome to the final book in my Guardians, Inc., series, *Bodyguard Reunion.* I have enjoyed coming up with various stories revolving around female bodyguards. When I came up with this series, I wanted to showcase tough women who loved God and yet could be totally feminine when they wanted to. What a nice way to end the series, with a male and female bodyguard having to team up and protect a couple in jeopardy.

I love hearing from readers. You can contact me at margaretdaley@gmail.com or at 1316 S. Peoria Ave., Tulsa, OK 74120. You can also learn more about my books at www.margaretdaley.com. I have a quarterly newsletter that you can sign up for on my website, or you can enter my monthly drawings by signing my guest book on the website.

Best wishes,

Margaret Daley

Questions for Discussion

1. Trust is important in a relationship. Both T.J. and Chloe had a hard time trusting people because of the nature of being professional bodyguards. Has anyone caused you to distrust him/her? Why?

2. Chloe was self-reliant, but when she and T.J. protected the Zimmermans, they both had to learn to depend on each other. Is it possible to go through life not needing anyone? Who do you depend on and why?

3. T.J. was at a crossroads in his life. Have you ever been at a crossroads in your life? How did you resolve it?

4. Chloe chose to stay in Texas rather than follow T.J. to Washington, D.C., because her mother was ill with cancer. After her mother got better, Chloe didn't join him in Washington. Have you ever been afraid to make a commitment to something or

someone? What did you do about it? Any regrets about your decision?

5. T.J. was disillusioned by some of the things he saw as a Secret Service agent. Have you ever been disillusioned by someone's behavior? How did you handle it?

6. Mary and Paul Zimmerman's lives were turned upside down when someone tried to kill them. When life seems impossible, what do you do? Who do you turn to for help?

7. Aaron was angry with his parents and their busy work schedule. He sometimes felt isolated and alone. Do you have a teenage child? How do you spend time with them?

8. The villain of the book was motivated by greed and jealousy. Sometimes it is hard not to want what another has. How do you deal with these dark emotions?

9. Mary had a hard time believing someone wanted to kill her. She didn't know how to deal with it. What would you do if someone felt that kind of anger toward you?

REQUEST YOUR FREE BOOKS!

2 FREE INSPIRATIONAL NOVELS IN TRUE LARGE PRINT
PLUS 2 FREE MYSTERY GIFTS

YES! Please send me 2 FREE Love Inspired® True Large Print novels and my 2 FREE mystery gifts (gifts are worth about $10). After receiving them, if I don't wish to receive any more books, I can return the shipping statement marked "cancel." If I don't cancel, I will receive 3 brand-new true large print novels every month and be billed just $7.99 per book in the U.S. or $9.99 per book in Canada. That's a savings of at least 20% off the cover price. It's quite a bargain! Shipping and handling is just 50¢ per book in the U.S. and 75¢ per book in Canada.* I understand that accepting the 2 free books and gifts places me under no obligation to buy anything. I can always return the shipment and cancel at any time. Even if I never buy another book, the two free books and gifts are mine to keep forever.

117/317 IDN F5FZ

Name _____ (PLEASE PRINT)

Address _____ Apt. # _____

City _____ State/Prov. _____ Zip/Postal Code _____

Signature (if under 18, a parent or guardian must sign)

Mail to the **Harlequin® Reader Service:**
IN U.S.A.: P.O. Box 1867, Buffalo, NY 14240-1867
IN CANADA: P.O. Box 609, Fort Erie, Ontario L2A 5X3

* Terms and prices subject to change without notice. Prices do not include applicable taxes. Sales tax applicable in N.Y. Canadian residents will be charged applicable taxes. Offer not valid in Quebec. This offer is limited to one order per household. Not valid for current subscribers to Love Inspired True Large Print books. All orders subject to credit approval. Credit or debit balances in a customer's account(s) may be offset by any other outstanding balance owed by or to the customer. Please allow 4 to 6 weeks for delivery. Offer available while quantities last.

Your Privacy—The Harlequin® Reader Service is committed to protecting your privacy. Our Privacy Policy is available online at www.ReaderService.com or upon request from the Harlequin Reader Service.

We make a portion of our mailing list available to reputable third parties that offer products we believe may interest you. If you prefer that we not exchange your name with third parties, or if you wish to clarify or modify your communication preferences, please visit us at www.ReaderService.com/consumerschoice or write to us at Harlequin Reader Service Preference Service, P.O. Box 9062, Buffalo, NY 14269. Include your complete name and address.

LITLP13TRR